WHO WAS VIST?

Book 4 in the WHO IS VIST series

ANKA B. TROITSKY

January 2025

(This book contains scenes of grief)

Copyright © 2025 Anka B. Troitsky
Published in the UK by Greystone
Consultancy LTD
ISBN: 978-1-7391959-6-0

To those who inspired me all my life.

CONTENTS

Epigraph

I don't hate my spectacles, but the fact
that

I am too dependent on a pair of lenses,

without which I feel helpless, is worse
than being blind.

Friend's letters, 2006.

Why would you want to battle aliens
on another planet

when the planet itself can put up a
fight?.

Dad, 1985.

1 Part 1. The Colony of Continent Gera

They didn't return – none of them. The colony would never have been the same without those loaders. It cannot afford to lose the last ones.

The temple's high priest of O'Teka, the Architexter Timofey Hesley – the most complex loader ever – and his brother-in-law, Master Nathaniel Alloyway, sat above clouds in the highest chambers of the spear and looked at Noverca's sun, Vitricus. Or just Vitr. There was an eclipse, and the dark shape of the moon appeared to swallow the small red dwarf above the south horizon with great effort.

They did not say anything to each other or point to the few new stars in the amethyst sky, which became visible only during this rare occurrence. They did not turn once to look through the huge window behind them and to acknowledge the brightest dance of the Northern Lights. They could not hear the noise of the Schwarz Moon Festival far beneath their feet, on the lower platforms of the temple and the streets of the city. They sat in chairs facing the transparent wall, sipping their beer and waiting for this spectacular cosmic show to be over.

The Novercian moon is slow, so Nat was the first to get bored. He brushed back his long white hair and said, "Explain to me again, Tim. No matter how much I try, I can't reason with this. Why did Vist take no one but Mik to their search mission? Don't tell me it was her idea of a honeymoon."

"Her?"

Nat turned away from the purple smirk. "Oh, please don't start."

"It was my fault, Nat." Timofey's voice was full of serenity.

Nat, in contrast, felt the alcohol pushing him into a sulky and whiny mood. "But initially, you didn't plan to build the submarine so damn small!"

Tim answered patiently in his usual lecturer's manner. "Indeed, the necessity for modifications to *Marlin*'s design arose during the development process, with many of these adjustments proposed by the skilled Master McLeod. It's essential to remember that this was my inaugural project, shortly after my first upload. Additionally, we were constructing a

3

podvodlod, not a simple submarine. I have learned you had such incredible deep transport on Earth after the thirty-first century. Those vessels never exceeded the size of a train car, even when utilising converters for propulsion. While the perpetual light on our planet allowed for a slight increase in size, the living quarters remained too small to accommodate a sizeable crew due to the structure's need to withstand the water pressure."

Nat shook his head, lost halfway through that speech. "Yes – yes, I remembered you two arguing. But how could you let old Baker down? Vist practically uploaded to you everything Rod had in his head."

"Rod Baker didn't think so. The only unhappy and almost affronted person was you."

"Me? Well, because I didn't understand a single thing about that engine, and I am a pilot! I thought you were aiming for another avion."

"Vist believed it to be a coherent choice to traverse the ocean waters employing watercraft. The closest continent lies nearly seventeen thousand kilometres distant. On Earth, you had one ocean of such immense breadth" – Timofey coughed awkwardly – "when there was Earth. I am sorry."

Nat put the empty bottle on the low table and stretched his legs. "You guys built the craziest thing ever. I am not used to that. I must know everything about the machine I am driving."

"Perhaps that's the reason Vist chose to pilot *Marlin* personally. However, it's evident that your present resentment is primarily directed at the others. Isn't it? You're the one who feels a sense of injustice. A few years later, you felt betrayed by your former mentor for training a new pilot for the latest avion. Then, by my sister, who decided to become pregnant and carry your baby herself, coinciding with the time of the rescue team selection last year."

Nat did not answer. After a minute, he said quietly, "She didn't do it deliberately."

"Talking about your wife, where is Andrea now?"

"At Larsson's hotel in Pettogreco. She took the kids to your mother to experience the 'earthly night' show with fireworks and everything. It's much darker in those regions right now, you know."

"Yes, I know. It would be in your best interest to join your family," Timofey replied. "I would have liked to do the same. Still, I find myself bound to the temple during the party, as an overwhelming workload awaits me once the festivities conclude." He double-tapped his foot against the floor, referring to the celebrating crowd on the square.

Both got up and said goodbye in O'Teka fashion. Nat bent slightly to touch Timofey's purple forehead with his own. He lightly squeezed both round shoulders as if apologising for his grumpy mood during the festival.

"Thank you for keeping me company this cycle," Timofey said, sitting back down and opening another bottle.

Nat entered the lift.

On the way down, he remembered what had happened eleven months ago. Four of his friends had disappeared off the radar, almost exactly like Vist and Mik nine years ago.

When enough time passed without a word from Vist, a search mission was attempted. Rod and Steven took a few more years to build Noverca's newest and most advanced avion, *Skippers*. Colonial engineers and the best technology designer companies helped, but not much. This project wasn't commercial; the lack of needed materials and funds was significant. And although everyone missed the first architexter, Vist, no one believed in his or her survival, apart from the rest of the loaders and their friends.

***

It was a chain of unfortunate events that started a long time ago. More than a generation back, *Wasp*, the WSP-class spacecraft that brought its crew from the lost planet Earth, travelled south-west. It had to investigate the strange appearance of a new island at the very edge of the range of a geostationary satellite. It was a time when the *Wasp* no longer travelled through wormholes and only climbed into orbit to launch and maintain the satellite. Still, it was indispensable for scientific research expeditions and rescue missions. Only her pilot Nat and Captain Tom Darkwood were aboard the old spaceship that cycle. Nat returned from that expedition alone.

The ship's cameras added to his story the recording of a terrible murky sea funnel from which Tom did not emerge. Then, everyone except Vist was sure that he was dead. Vist reminded everyone that in one of the legends on Earth, it was repeatedly described how, mistaking a sea monster for an island, sailors landed on it. They never returned to their ship, but later, they reappeared alive by some miracle. In this case, the architexter ruled out any miracles and stated that, first, Tom was in a bio-suit. Second, Tom was not a mere mortal, but a loader, that is, a person whose organism, including the central nervous system, was significantly enhanced by the most advanced neuroware and loaded with data that increases his chance of survival where even a native Novercian would not survive despite genetic modifications. They must wait and watch out, and Tom would find a way to make himself known. Nat regularly flew out in search of Tom for several more years but only circled over that sector and around for a long time, scanning the ocean depths in search of the captain's amulet, but he did not find a trace to cling to.

Tom's friends, his wife Zina, and their son grieved and waited, but Vist didn't just wait. Vist was counting on watching out in their own way. Every year, they launched into orbit above the troposphere, another link of ozoniser – a hexagonal ring, a segment in the gradually growing net around the main satellite directly above the spear of the Temple of O'Teka. An artificially created umbrella of ozone, called O-zont, protected the colony from radiation as efficiently as a protective field over cities. In a couple of generations, it was supposed to cover the entire central region of the Gera continent, eventually producing enough for the whole planet. But since the day Captain Darkwood disappeared, Vist's apprentice Timofey Hesley noticed that instead of being evenly distributed over the temple, joining the network, new segments somehow started to spread in a particular direction. Timofey didn't tell anyone about this but questioned his master. Vist explained that there was indeed a deliberate attempt to stretch the satellite viewing area as far as possible to the south-west, where beyond islands lay the edge of the first large continent, about which there was still no information except for scans and images taken from orbit by the *Wasp*.

Timofey's life gained new purpose. Being in a high position in the temple, he worked the most with the satellite anyway. On that cycle, he was also tasked with carefully monitoring visual signals from the south-western edge of the ozoniser network, specially equipped with scanners and instruments that searched for impulses of Tom's amulet, emitted even if its owner was dead. Timofey also wanted to find Captain Darkwood and carefully studied those scanners' records thrice a week. He had little hope, especially since it became clear that new segments would not be launched into orbit any more. During an incident in the permafrost, when Vist almost died, the old *Wasp* fell through the ice. There were no other spaceships on Noverca.

Timofey Hesley was always very persistent, to the point of obsession. When he finally found what he sought, Tim showed Vist the data taken from the satellite. Vist announced that Timofey was now ready to become a top-loader himself, becoming the chief priest of the temple and helping Vist to save Thomas Darkwood. With his contribution to the design and construction of a new transport, rescuers could go in search of Tom in just a few cycles.

Timofey's body withstood the upload, but it took longer to recover from shock than he had hoped. Choosing the right type of transport was also difficult. With the help of the legendary engineer Rodion Baker, who decided it was too early for him to die, the underwater vessel, the podvodlod *Marlin*, was created.

Vist and Mik launched on it towards the only sign that Tom was alive. There, far in the south-west, in the waters of the intercontinental ocean, one satellite segment spotted a strange object that could only be sent by a human and only by an earthling. After all, it was also addressed to an earthling familiar with the message-in-a-bottle concept. To send it, someone beyond the horizon carefully timed a regular southern hot storm, which brought a large buoy into the waters of the Galtstream. It was a salt sphere made by a certain sea creature but painted in colours never seen by people in the Novercian sky – the colours of a rainbow.

***

Nat left the temple and stood for some time in the square, which was getting brighter every minute. The protective dome had already switched off the transparency and begun to project thick clouds, hiding the unmovable and once-again-bright Vitr, indicating the approaching resting hours. The fireworks had already ended, but the groups of dancing townspeople had only now begun to thin out and move towards their streets. The music playing in many amulets also gradually faded away. Hatches opened in the surface of the square, from which robotic janitors rose, but were in no hurry to begin their duties, as if waiting for people to go home. Nat sat on a bench under a rowan tree with blood-red berries and activated his amulet. He opened the file with the log of those events a few years back. At that time, those events filled the local news broadcasts with almost daily scoops.

By the time the mysterious buoy reached the equator riding the stream, the podvodlod was almost ready. Steven McLeod fished out the coloured orb with a diameter of about forty centimetres on his yacht before the current turned north and carried it away from Gera.

He brought it to the port, where he was greeted by a huge crowd as if he had found an alien spaceship or the sea beast, possibly responsible for Tom's disappearance.

Vist was most interested in the chemical composition of the paint used to decorate the salt ball because it could say much about Tom's abilities.

Even Mik, who knew Vist best, couldn't tell whether the loader was disappointed or impressed as he or she looked back at the dear friends and said, "I suspected so. It is an organic pigment! And it's waterproof."

No blobster's salt sphere has ever been studied so scrupulously. Centimetre by centimetre, a working group from the temple laboratory scrutinised and analysed the smooth surface. But they only found a shallow cavity the size of a fingernail. Tom would not punch a hole in the hollow ball because water could get into it and drown it. But he made a small depression chiselled out by a hard object. But what for?

One of the researchers wrote the following in his offering to O'Teka: "A few remaining particles indicate that the cavity was made with a piece of slate and then sealed with resin from the seaweed *resinae cingulum*. Mr Darkwood knew it wouldn't dissolve in water. Still, he apparently did not know that its natural decomposer is a microorganism that lives in colder regions, away from the latitude where we assume he is trapped. We can only guess what he tried to seal in this cavity as the content washed out. Apart from amino acid fragments in the porous wall, nothing remained. My theory is that he was trying to send his DNA. Maybe a hair or a sample of his flesh. I thought at first that this could be the amino acids of the blobster that created the sphere, but we did not find it anywhere else in the sphere but that cavity."

So, Tom somehow survived for years beyond the sea. Vist could not miss that opportunity to find out how. Bringing Tom back became a priority. Everyone was excited about Tom returning home, including his wife, Dr Zina, although she had moved on with her life and remarried.

Nat looked around the empty and quiet square, raised the larger holo-screen in the air and scrutinised the image of the vessel built for the mission. Then he looked at the last picture of Mik and Vist next to it for a long time.

Marlin was a small and fast podvodlod, the type of submarine that resembles the flier-pods but for deep waters, not wormholes. Only Mik accompanied Vist in their journey this time. Everyone knew by then that these two had started a romantic relationship since their last adventure. The new couple always rested either in Mik's house or Vist's mansion. During all common gatherings, Mik sat next to Vist, not in his usual darkest corner. Both were loaders and spoke to each other mostly by touching hands. The look on Vist's face during those times convinced many people that Vist was a woman. Nevertheless, even natural curiosity died out among their friends after many years of wondering. Vist was just Vist. Everyone had got used to that by then.

As soon as *Marlin* left the satellite's coverage area, Vist and Mik seemed to disappear from the face of Noverca. Neither the promised robotic postman from the architexter nor another message in a bottle reached the colony.

***

Nat flipped through his notes on the following rescue plan and saw a new message from Obydva. An old friend invited him to the Bakers' residence, where he lived with his children in the absence of old Rod Baker. The house was only a few minutes' walk away. Nat quickly checked on Andrea and the children and hurried to Buckthorn Street.

There, he was met by Rod's daughter Phoebe and her husband, who were setting the table. Phoebe considered Obydva her second father, but not because his genetic material was used to create her.

Obydva Grinsky was a special loader, a fusion of two distinct individuals. His body was once the mighty Tolyan Grin, the rebel soldier from Earth, whose head and spine now housed the neuroware of the brave pilot Marta Larsson-Broadsky, uploaded by Vist himself. Marta, a courageous pilot, had fallen victim to a true monster in human form. Thus, Obydva became the second loader on Noverca, sharing the same loves and loyalties as his donors, perhaps because they were not as dissimilar as one might think. This newly formed loader possessed a unique personality and embarked on a brand-new life. Loaders possess a wide range of abilities, but when it comes to emotions and knowledge, they're capable of things that regular folks can't even begin to grasp.

Obydva was neither Marta nor Tolyan. He remembered and loved everything Marta remembered and loved, but fragments of Tolyan's memory and inclinations were also present. Obydva still resembled Tolyan but was no longer a huge strongman with a rude sense of humour. His attachment to the Baker family was not entirely explainable. Ten years ago, he found Marta's genetic contribution in the gene bank, rented an artificial womb from the Carib Clinic on Pettogreco and acquired the son he had long dreamed of. But with little Dmitro, he brought home a second baby named Yar'oma, whose origins only three other people knew about. To any questions about the second child, Obydva answered: "No, he is not mine, at least genetically. But he is an orphan and *my* responsibility now." Others said they were bound by a vow of silence given to Obydva and the Architexter Vist, so the questions eventually stopped.

"Papa is upstairs trying to get the little ones to sleep," Phoebe said and nodded towards the stairs leading to the second floor. She was as tall as Obydva and had the same light brown hair twisted into three long braids.

Nat slowly went up and heard a low howl that was supposed to be the lullaby from Earth: "A little cherry tree trembles by the window. It is asking to come in because winter has come."

Nat approached the doorway and peered in. The room was darkened, with one holo-window projecting an image of Earth's sea with a full moon above and its pathlike reflection in the water. Obydva sat in the chair between two beds. The boy on his left was asleep, but on his right, the purple-skinned child opened his eyes and looked at Nat. His eyes reflected the light of the holographic moon and appeared to glow by themselves.

Obydva stopped singing. "You are here. Good," he said quietly, got up and headed towards the door.

"Yar'oma is still awake," Nat noted.

"He will stay awake for half the sleep time," Obydva replied, "I hoped he would get used to going to bed earlier, but the only progress so far is that he dozes off at three, not five."

Obydva closed the door, and both friends went downstairs to the dining room, where the table was ready. When Nat sat down, Phoebe put the plate before him and said, "This is goulash. I am sorry, I didn't get any fresh dill. It just would not grow in our garden."

"No worries," said Nat, taking the first mouthful and closing his eyes. "Mmm. Delicious!"

Obydva chuckled and said, "Yes, she is getting pretty good at cooking meat. Elya, please pass me the cheese flakes. Thanks."

Phoebe's husband, Elya Goryn, wasn't very talkative, but Nat guessed that he shared the meal with them this time for a reason. Nat moved his gaze to the place at the table that had remained unoccupied for almost a year. It was Rod Baker's, a good spot for his wheelchair at some point, but after becoming a loader, he didn't need the wheel's help any more. He regained his health and became strong and witty once again, but he still looked like a skinny grey elder. Nat was chewing on his food, but his thoughts were with Rod. The old friend worked nonstop; he sold everything he had except for this house, but it still took him a few years to build an avion capable of flight across the sea. Others helped, but the legendary engineer mostly relied on his lady friend, an old widow, Lariona Parera, for inspiration and significant funds. Rod's daughters suspected there was a certain background that bonded them.

By the time the avion was ready, Obydva had completed the training for the new pilot. Phoebe's sister Groonya was supposed to become a second pilot to Nat. Obydva and Rod determined that ordinary flying academy cadets from the colony could not be trusted with a new machine. But just a week before the expedition, Andrea dropped the bomb on Nat. His lovely wife made it clear that she would not use an artificial womb and, therefore, couldn't go with him or let him go. All she could do, being the rare specialist in travelling equipment, was to help equip those who were going. So eleven months ago, *Skippers* dived into a thick blanket of orange clouds and left geostationary satellite coverage in less than an hour. It was piloted by Groonya Baker, accompanied by her first father, Rod Baker, and by the McLeod couple, Steven and Dr Zina.

Nat again stayed behind to receive a new kid. Obydva also said that his boys were too young and too special to be raised by anybody else.

Soon after, the lone and well-charged "postman" the size of a monkfish crossed the intercontinental ocean and activated the silent beacon less than a kilometre from the port. The message was recorded in Rod's usual manner:

"Oi, Obydva, Tim and Nat.

"Just to let you know, we're halfway to our destination and all tickety-boo in here, but we haven't found any signs of human activity yet. Now,

there's something you ought to know. The info about the undercurrent nearby is a bit out of date. The current's faster than the Wasp measured, and the water is cooler than previously thought. So, things aren't as dodgy as we expected. The air's only forty-two degrees Celsius, so we're considering checking out the nearest chain of islands.

"No signs of a submarine or the presence of loaders have yet been detected, although Zina suspects that some signals are trying to break through. We are fine. Apart from lack of sleep and strange dreams, nothing concerns us.

"The flight was a breeze, and I'm fit as a fiddle. Zina, Groonya and Steven send their love. Groonya wants you to remind Jaxon not to forget to take Cora to the temple on Fridays, and she thanks Obydva for all the help.

"Rod, over and out."

This positive message was followed by a medical report from Dr Zina on the crew's condition. Nothing serious except for sleep disturbances, but it was too early to conclude.

That relaxed everyone, but Obydva and Nat were the first to start worrying again. Nothing else came from either of the parties. Nat had no patience left. He was a great pilot, but he could not build ships. A few months later, when Obydva got tired of Nat's constant complaints, he stood up to his full, gigantic height over him. Reminding Nat of Tolyan's Russian accent, he bellowed, "What makes you think I'm just sitting on my hands here? I can't stand it when you constantly breathe down my neck! If you don't stop, I'll leave you behind. Remember, I'm a good pilot, too. Be patient, and I'll call you when everything's ready."

Nat finished his goulash, took his glass of wine and stared at Obydva. What did they used to say back on Earth? Today is the day. Right?

Obydva glared from under his brows and said, "I can't build new transport of such calibre without Steven."

Nat sighed and put the glass back on the table. "Then I'll take his yacht. If I manage to get to the first island, there will be a whole chain of —"

"Wait! Let me finish. Elya's department and I built something else. A disposable aircrane, using old Rod's blueprints from when we searched for missing pods. Rod wanted to use the same manual control mechanism as in his tetrahoders on Earth. You will fly to a new continent on the *Wasp*."

Nat couldn't believe his ears.

"What?"

"Look, Master Alloyway." Elya activated his amulet and projected the screen above the table. Nat saw a terrible-looking construction resembling a Chinook thermocopter and a long-legged fly at the same time.

Obydva crossed his arms. "Don't you dare laugh at it! This machine is the only thing that can help us now. You will have one shot at it. If you fail, you will have an emergency battery, just enough to return and recharge before trying again. The energy needed to cut out a spaceship from ice and then carry it back is more than ZPE converters can get from the environment so far north."

"I get it," Nat replied, squinting at the rotating image. "What do those legs do? Grab things? Oh, Teka! Those blades are massive?"

"Yes, and our *Wasp* is heavy. She is much bigger than those tiny pods you used to recover from the ice," Obydva said, turning to Elya. "Show him. It's your baby after all."

Master Goryn lifted both hands and enlarged the image to almost take up the whole room. "The credit is not mine. I am an amulet designer, but one of my regular customers sent me two of his best engineers from the cargo-handling service. They worked in my department for a few months, and Mrs Parera contributed greatly to reward them for their efforts. The engine, arms, blades, rotors and shafts were tested on one of the borrowed passenger's avions on the cargo port, where it awaits you now. A large amount of power will be needed to lift and carry the *Wasp* and produce enough heat to free her. The power beam will not cut out the ship but melt the ice around it. The *Wasp* is not sitting too deep. Then, we can bring her to the surface using the power scoop, and these arms will hold her all the way to the port. They work on the same principle as a third limb model by Mrs Alloyway."

"Six oversized synthetic tentacles. Clever!" Nat rubbed his palms together, "When can I go?"

Obydva nodded to Elya, and he turned the screen off.

"When you're ready," Obydva said, "Nat, you must promise you will take care of this crane. We will need it again after you get the *Wasp*. That ZPE converter was the most expensive part and was purchased only after a few Nordian families of deceased seismologists chipped in to pay for it on one condition. You will lift their drowned avion from the ice, too. It's right next to the *Wasp* and might have some bodies of their brothers inside. I promised Mik to do that, but that was before I lost my Bumblebag avion."

"I'll do my best," said Nat.

At this moment, Nat felt like it was his birthdate and he was ready to promise anything to anyone.

***

"Ahhh, baby. That's it! Sweet girl, I can see your bottom already! Yes! Yes! I miss you so much. Come to Daddy ... That's it. I will call this aircrane Daddy." Nat almost wept when he saw a familiar figure on the screen, hanging in a ball of tentacles that were still moving, as if alive, groping and wrapping around the hull of a small spaceship.

The control cabin was cold, causing Nat's long eyelashes to become white, thick and heavy. Outside the lone window, the temperature plummeted to minus fifty-eight degrees Celsius. The sky was cloudless and adorned with stars, creating the impression that the air across the world was as frigid as the vastness of space. Exhaling into it seemed to shatter the air into a multitude of icy particles, glinting in the light of the immense moon. Just above the mountains, the hunched yellow figures of the Northern Lights meandered across the sky. Meanwhile, the horizon appeared to the south as a luminous thread, arrow-straight. Disturbed by the thermocopter's rotating blades, the grey masses of snowdrifts reluctantly ascended, transforming into dense smoke dispersing in every direction.

Nat carefully raised his left hand in a glove entangled with wires, moved it to the side a few centimetres, and felt the aerial crane swing a few metres to the south. He looked up and saw copter blades flashing through the observation window. Nat couldn't hear them. He carefully lowered the *Wasp* onto the snow, and while waiting for as much water as possible to leak out of it, a not entirely rational idea occurred to him. The process he had just completed brought him so much pleasure and joy that he could not resist and returned to the giant hole he had created in the ice. The water on the surface had already calmed down and was beginning to form a thin crust of ice. He remembered this place too well, and his anxiety, when he saw wild creatures on that slope and when he did not find either Vist or the *Wasp*. He felt so all alone at the time.

A few minutes later, Nat heard Timofey's voice in his earpiece, "Nat, what are you doing? Are you crazy?"

"Calm down. This avion is small and quite close to the surface. Not much left."

"I thought so. You're melting the ice over it, aren't you? Stop it at once! Heat requires much more energy than lifting weights."

"I know, but it's a trifle. If I stop, it will freeze again. Let's not let the goodness go to waste now."

"I don't believe it! What do you think Vist would have said?"

Nat extinguished the beam and brought his free right hand to his face. It's a good thing he remembered not to make any movements with his left hand. The whole operation would have come to an end if he had.

Unbelievable!

What happened to him over the last few years? He considered himself the best student of the high loader when it came to logic, reasoning, calculations, solving problems and unravelling mysteries. Is it possible that without the direct influence of the architexter, he let himself go and turned into a capricious whiner? He knew very well what Vist would have said: *A person of integrity remains truthful and steadfast in their principles, even in solitude, when there is no external scrutiny.*

"I hope I didn't ruin everything." Nat scolded himself for being weak-hearted for a minute, returned to the ship and released the tentacles again. He lifted the ship thirty metres above the ground and headed south towards the golden horizon, carrying his precious burden above the rocks.

Obydva, to whom Timofey had vented his frustrations, was already yelling and cursing Nat in his earpiece. If not for the emergency batteries and the clear weather in the area where the ZPEC began eagerly absorbing Vitr's radiation, the pilot might not have reached the warm zone and would have risked freezing.

Obydva waited at the port.

Lifted off the ground by his collar with two strong hands, Nat said quickly, "*Wasp*'s ZPEC is still intact. I could feel it almost as soon as it emerged from the salty water. It's more potent and could recharge both ships in case of a problem." Obydva waggled his eyebrows, released Nat and slapped him on the back of the head. Marta used to do this when she was alive, and Nat was in his twenties.

***

"I have found your recent behaviour concerning. You've become unreliable, and while perhaps Andrea tolerates it at home, in our search enterprise – which might be the last chance for our friends – I can no longer place absolute trust in you. Maybe in a few years, I'll gather the necessary funds to attempt to find them myself. However, besides Obydva and me, no one else on Noverca believes in the possibility of finding them alive. Even after encountering that orb, which could have been a message from Tom or something else entirely, there remains a chance that our interpretation was incorrect. Therefore, whether you argue or not, I won't let you go alone. You will take at least two people, preferably with good training and impeccable integrity."

Nat didn't argue with Tim, the architexter. Instead, he pondered over whom to enlist from his regular search team. This upcoming journey would be perilous, necessitating an upfront and substantial reward for any native resident of the colony. He could call for volunteers, and several potential names crossed his mind. However, he hesitated to invite anyone to follow him to the location from which neither he nor they might return. Initially, he had contemplated going on the *Wasp* alone, but Andrea's plea aligned with her brother's resolution and persuaded Nat to reconsider. She wanted him to return even if he failed to find the missing people.

But he didn't have to worry about this for long. Four scouts entered the official meeting room on the nineteenth floor of the temple on Timofey's invitation. Nat knew these people well. All were descendants of the first generation of colonists, except one. All were at least fifty years old, but they looked like true representatives of new genetically improved races, just as if they were in their thirties. These four were volunteers from his last search party, during which he explored the western group of islands for ores and especially rare bauxites. They managed to get into a little trouble in those waters without casualties, but since then, all four have often said they like adventures more than simple tests of new technology on Gera.

All four were masters of three to six different professions and good pilots, especially

Hans Korub, the Terenian with dark purple skin and white eyes. His partner, Nelia Korub, was responsible for the tech-maintenance during all expeditions. Her skin was lighter, and her face shimmered on her cheekbones and forehead with pearlescent scales inherited from her Uzhan mother. Her thick black hair and muscular stature spoke of Nordian blood. Another woman, a medical officer, entered the room after her. Irida Pavlovic was born into the Ikhtees family, but in her youth, she decided to fly, not swim and after several operations, she returned from the sea to land. Her origin was revealed only by the absence of hair and the membranous crest on her head. The last was the youngest scout in the group, flexible and fast; the earthling Naoki Endo still suffered from a lack of violet protective pigment and was forced to undergo gland transplantation every few years. His ivory skin was rougher than the thin dermis of Novercians, and his eyes struggled in the Gera twilight zone, but in the south lands, he saw better than the others.

Timofey waited silently, his hands folded over his round belly, his face conveying just one word: *choose.*

Nat surveyed all four of them and immediately decided to bring the earthling along. Given Naoki's physiology, Nat wouldn't have to worry about him sustaining injuries in case of another fall. Naoki had been the first to recover after the previous disaster. Irida, despite losing her amphibian abilities, remained a valuable comrade, particularly in aquatic environments. Nat addressed the Korub couple. "Last time, we nearly perished because, Nelia, you were more concerned about your husband than about yourself and the others. Should I risk something like that again?"

Nelia held her gaze and responded with conviction. "Sir, you're right and I wouldn't trust myself in that situation again. However, we were informed that there was a possibility we might not return from overseas, just like the ancient loaders. If so, we'd prefer to be lost together."

Nat met Hans's pearly eyes, seemingly blind but perceptive in their own way.

"Yes, sir," Hans replied, affirming the unspoken question.

"I won't waste time questioning why you want to participate in this mission," Nat declared, turning to everyone. "I have nothing to pay you with this time. I'm confident that Architexter Vist will compensate you fully if we find her, but I understand your motives. The thrill is infectious, and you can't experience it anywhere in tranquil Gera. Since it was my fault that you tasted it in the first place, I'll take all of you. Be ready by 9 a.m. on Tuesday. You will receive your gear from Mrs Alloyway's warehouse in the cycle before that."

He turned and went to check on Obydva, who was about to return from orbit on the good old *Wasp*. After all, the production of ozone producers had not stopped in the last ten years since that ship went missing, and O-zont's network now extended further south-west for as many as ten hexagons.

Part 2. *Marlin* **the Podvodlod**

It was a push. Barely tangible, like a random accidental touch in a crowd. But the sensors of the underwater vessel were programmed to diligently avoid all obstacles without changing course, and neither aquatic plants nor blobsters nor their spheres nor drifting ice could be a reason for such a collision.

Mik King didn't feel that push. He was fast asleep, lying on his stomach with his right arm hanging to the floor. But Vist felt it. The loader carefully slipped out from under Mik's left arm and got up. A liquid-like matter enveloped the smooth pale body within a few seconds, instantly turning into a soft black and silver fabric. Inside the podvodlod there was no one except the two of them, and Vist did not need the long robe. It was stored in the luggage niche for the journey to the hot places of the new continent and for returning. That is if they would ever return to Gera. For this journey, Vist was wearing only a bio-suit, necessary for navigation and vessel control.

The *Marlin* was a small and cosy podvodlod. On the outside, it was not much bigger than a city double-deck conmot. There were no more than seven to ten steps from the two suites at the back to the control room at the front.

Vist approached the controls and raised both hands. A horseshoe-shaped screen immediately rose into the air above the panel and surrounded the loader. Numerous cameras on the ship's shell projected a detailed view of its environment, but nothing was visible besides the thick and nearly opaque, plankton-filled water. Just like yesterday and just like the day they crossed the equator.

Vist twitched their left thumb, and the ship sent an ultrasonic wave in the direction from which the disturbance was received. But there was nothing there. Vist repeated the call, this time in all directions around the ship, including above and under it. On the screen, instead of an image of plankton masses, a sonar reading grid appeared, and it was then that Vist saw a colossal figure slowly moving away about half a kilometre lower than the ship and further west. It seemed that whatever it was, it had also sensed the ultrasonic signal because it immediately increased its speed and disappeared from the sonar's echolocation range.

From behind, Vist heard the sound of barefoot walking, and a tall, naked Mik stood by Vist's shoulder, rubbing his eyes.

"Well, I'll be damned. Show me that fish again, gorgeous," he said, skipping all the unnecessary questions.

Vist replayed the reading of what Mik called "that fish" and paused it, highlighting and isolating the image, increasing it and enhancing it to the most likely three-dimensional shape. Vist's arms relaxed. Now both were looking at an elongated form, somewhat similar to an eel, but shorter, with a laterally compressed body and large dorsal and ventral fins ending in filaments, giving it a double-sided comb shape. There was something that resembled a pelvic fin, but it was long like a whip and jagged.

"What the hell is this?" Mik asked, "It's definitely not an overgrown blobster. Is this thing a living organism?"

"Even blobsters have a two-chambered organ that functions as a heart. I didn't hear anything like a pulse here," answered Vist.

"But then what? We've never seen anything like this before. Or even heard of it."

Vist closed their eyes. "You're wrong, dear. Remember our very first day on Noverca, when we read the reports of the pioneers from *Noah-8*? They never sailed this far to the northwest again after something "pierced" their submarine's external layer. They called the incident a "dragon attack," although this thing looks to me more like a long-extinct earthly creature, *Idiacanthus*, but without a head. The huge teethmarks on *Noah*'s covering were quite far apart."

"I don't see a toothy mouth either, and we are not in northern waters. What makes you think this *is* the dragon?"

"Mik, I don't know what Tom would have called this creature, but I will catalogue it as a *sine capite draco*."

"A headless dragon? Ha! Can you measure it up?" Mik put his hands on Vist's shoulders.

Vist paused for a second and replied, "I am using your usual scout equation, taking into account the sonar readings and my own senses. The creature is almost 179 metres long. The whip – let's call it that – is 33 metres long and appears to be very muscular. The distance between the teeth on the whip is 13.8 cm, the teeth themselves are 29.2 cm long, and the distance between the tips of the teeth can vary because the whip can bend. I still think such a tool can be useful only to a living creature."

"To catch blobsters?" Mik raised his hand and motioned as if grabbing something out of the air.

"Perhaps. We know so little about food chains in areas far from Gera. A blobster isn't an apex predator, as some unknown factor controls their population. As for the latitude of the habitat, it is impossible to conclude anything after just three encounters."

"Three? Are you saying that Tom became a victim of this ... dragon? Could the *Wasp* really land on it? Let me see Nat's recording once more."

Vist raised their hand again, and the image on the concave screen changed. Now, it showed the landscape of a flat, probably about 200 metres long, narrow isle along which a man was walking. That man was Captain Tom. He walked further and further away, accompanied by Nat's comments. The pilot recorded this event on his amulet from inside the *Wasp*. Soon, the recording of Nat's cameras switched to Tom's, looking under his feet and at the peculiar broad slabs leading down to the water gradually. The whole island seemed to consist only of this wide staircase with flat and low steps.

Mik and Vist once again saw Tom's boots and heard his voice. "A remarkable structure, abundant in silicon and carbon, challenges my initial belief that it's sandstone. Its surface is adorned with the desiccated foam of sea brine. While it could be a fossil, the slabs look too much like something crafted by human hands. Hey! What is this?"

The recording showed Tom squatting near a round formation between two diverging steps. It was a deep depression filled with some tangled black threads. Tom reached out his bio-suit-gloved hand and carefully touched the threads.

They moved. But Tom and the camera in his left pupil were no longer looking at the depression but forwards at the steps before him, which began to fold like fan blades and fall under the water one by one. Tom turned and ran towards the ship.

Then, the recording again showed what Nat saw. He shouted to Tom, "Run!" as he turned on the ZPE engines. The long island was becoming shorter with every second. The steps were disappearing under the water, with white-green foamy waves rising on both sides.

Tom didn't reach the *Wasp*. Nat barely had time to take off, seeing that his captain had disappeared under the water, as did the entire island a moment later. The *Wasp* hovered over the seething whirlpool, and even after the water calmed down, he hoped for a long time to hear

Tom's signals, catch his camera or see his floating body.

After a moment of silence, Mik said, "So it was this thing taking a nap on its side."

Vist brought up the image of the dragon and said, "Or it was sunbathing, recharging on the surface. We can only speculate about its physiology, but numerous ancient creatures on Noverca draw on radiation energy more than respiration. And this dragon looks very ancient indeed. It was here long before us. I think we can theorise now why it lacks a pulse, although it might possess some form of vascular network. This alien life is not an animal but something rather closer to flora than fauna."

"What? A plant?"

After integrating the images with the data from Tom's and Nat's records, the headless dragon on the screen looked more detailed.

"I always felt uneasy referring to the indigenous species here using terms for animals and plants. O'Teka's classification system provides names for the local kingdoms that were unfamiliar to us on Earth, at least in our era. I refer to this group as 'animophytes' – a term intended to encompass entities that exhibit characteristics of both animals and plants. They possess fusionchondrias and employ gammasynthesis to convert radiation into usable energy." Vist turned, their olive eyes lifting to meet Mik's gaze, who was on the verge of a yawn. "I can explain it to you; it's somewhat unrelated to the synthesis of metallic nanoparticles."

"No, no, my love . . . Ha ha ha! Biology lessons make me sleepy. Let's talk about it after breakfast. For now, I have a better idea." Mik effortlessly lifted Vist, pressed them against his chest and strolled back to the bedroom, laughter filling the air as Vist held on to his strong neck.

***

Despite the diversion from their original course, Vist and Mik decided to pursue the mysterious headless dragon. Intrigued by the creature that had touched their vessel and then retreated upon sensing the ultrasound signal, Vist made several assumptions about its behaviour. Feeling the excitement of the hunt, Mik questioned Vist's idea regarding the dragon's non-aggressive nature.

Vist explained, "Let's say it relies on several food sources. In addition, its fins, which look like a series of long fan blades, can filter plankton, like the whales of Earth did. It absorbs Vitr's energy but needs other minerals to make its proteins. I'm not sure if blobsters are part of its diet."

"But then why does it need a jagged whip? It doesn't seem to have anyone to defend itself from," asked Mik, who began to show interest in biology from a hunter's perspective.

"We don't know. Maybe it has a natural enemy. But the whip can also have peaceful functions. What if it's an organ of touch?"

"A hand with claws?"

"Well, yes. Or it digs with it. We don't know anything about its reproduction."

"But you have more than enough crazy theories," Mik said, laughing.

Two loaders had lived fairly close together in the confined space of the submarine for several days. It seemed to both that the air was electrified and full of mutual attraction, accompanied by the scent of honey wax, fresh sweat and wine. When surfacing once a cycle for ventilation and maintenance, to clean out the carbon dioxide filters and replenish the oxygen tanks, Vist humorously referred to it as a "honeymoon recess." Mik playfully declared the submarine wasn't small enough and Vist was still too far away.

Vist took charge of the controls, monitoring the external chemical detector. With the dragon so sensitive, the use of sonar was now deemed too risky. Following the trail of radioactive particles proved uncomplicated, and given the creature's likely habit of regularly surfacing, its body temperature would be higher than that of the surrounding depths. Within an hour, they located it, the dragon standing motionless a few long metres from the ocean floor.

Vist guided the *Marlin* as close as possible, almost brushing against a massive rock, then activated the external cameras. On the holo-screen, the dragon's peculiar form unfolded, swaying like a colossal kite, it's "whip" extending straight like a string from its midsection to the seabed.

Grinning, Vist remarked, "This is not only an organ of touch. This is an anchor."

"Is it . . . sleeping or something?" Mik asked.

"Maybe, but the opportunity to collect more information about the creature may not arise again. Mik, dear, you can programme the camera probe to swim along the body and back, taking as much data as possible, both visual and chemical. In the meantime, I'll try to figure out its internal structure."

They immediately set to work. A fish-like device separated from the boat and circled the dragon, transmitting information directly to the loader's spinal cord. Simultaneously, Vist created a three-dimensional model of the creature on a screen, detailing its internal and external anatomy.

Soon, Vist observed, "Mik, look at what an interesting nervous system our dragon has. Plants definitely don't have such a level of sensitivity. I don't see anything like a brain, though."

"No head, no brain," Mik quipped.

"There is a network of peripheral nerves and a dense cord of neurons running along the central column, but there is no spine as we know it. This long cord runs to . . . Mik, where is our probe now?"

"It just came back from the other end, and I am driving it down along the whip to take a closer look at the teeth."

After a short pause, Vist suddenly exclaimed, "Call it off . . . now!"

The huge body shuddered, teeth at the end of the whip, releasing the rock it clung to, and instantly clenching into a fist. The probe was crushed like a peanut, and small fragments surrounded this jagged knot in a silvery cloud.

Vist gasped as the image vanished from the holo-screen.

"It's time to leg it," said Mik.

"No, on the contrary. We must freeze and not move at all."

Mik whispered, as if the dragon could hear him, "Do you think it can see us?"

"It has no eyes, but ... it won't see us behind this rock if it uses ultrasound," Vist replied, activating the surface survey camera, extending slowly like an antenna above the rock.

The dragon, resembling a gigantic fringed ribbon, slowly tilted on one side and curled into a colossal upright column, like a rolled-up rug.

"Some kind of defence position?" Vist pondered. "It feels threatened by the unknown. I wonder what else can ever disturb its slumber."

"But why threatened?" Mik whispered. "The probe wasn't big enough."

"Maybe that's exactly why," Vist replied.

"Oh, I see what you mean. I would have freaked out, too, if I found a tiny fish in my bed."

"Look!" Vist exclaimed, pointing at the screen.

The toothy whip wriggled around the dragon, then stretched and started to approach their cover.

"It can sense us somehow," Mik said.

"It *is* time to leg it," said Vist, nodding as they lifted their left hand and made a circular motion with their right.

The podvodlod backed off, turned around and dived into the cloudlike mass of plankton above them. The loaders didn't witness how the end of the toothy whip touched the rock almost tenderly several times where the *Marlin* was hiding and then retreated in disappointment.

***

The trouble happened unexpectedly on the next cycle.

Mik watched with astonishment as the face he deemed the most beautiful suddenly transformed, acquiring a new and unfamiliar expression. Vist opened their eyes, and something similar to horror appeared within them.

"This is impossible," Vist uttered, almost in a whisper.

"Darling, what's wrong?" Mik also felt a sense of unease.

"Mik, I don't know, but I've never experienced anything like this."

Exactly a week had passed on the voyage, and Vist was preparing the first "swimming postman," which was supposed to reach the port at Pettogreco at the speed of a torpedo. Its purpose was to deliver the first report on their progress and an offering about the dragon to the O'Teka temple's archives. But the device was never launched.

They were both in a chamber that could serve several needs. The floor, walls and even the ceiling could be rotated and shifted, changing the interior. Depending on your choice, a small room could be turned into a refectory, a bedroom, a shower room or a cosy living room. This time, it was a gym, and just a minute ago, Mik was lifting weights and thinking to himself that he was having the happiest time of his life.

"What's the matter?" he asked again.

"I can't remember ... something important."

"Wait ... *You* can't remember? Are you unwell, my love?"

Vist's voice lost its confidence and almost pleaded, "I need to assess myself. I have a suspicion. I can't say for sure yet, but ... help me, Mik. Stop the submarine and ... find a way, motionless ... or ..."

The "swimming postman," which looked like a cannon-shaped shell with a tail, fell out of the architexter's hands and rolled under the massage bench.

Mik was horrified to witness the sudden dimming of Vist's olive eyes, which now stared through him with an empty and meaningless expression. It wasn't a state of sleep or unconsciousness; it was something else. Unlike other loaders, Vist heavily relied on the bio-suit, an autonomous system capable of deciding how to protect the body in times of danger. Mik recalled a previous incident where Vist fell through the ice, and the suit, in response, had suspended vital functions to preserve the loader in a dormant state for a long time.

Despite Vist's current signs of life – breathing, a beating heart, blinking, and responses to external stimuli – the cognitive functions responsible for information storage appeared inexplicably switched off.

Mik could not tell if it was the bio-suit's doing or whether something was truly wrong with Vist. He decided not to waste time but to contemplate, systematically considering the possibilities. His extensive field experience taught him to remain calm and rational, even as his fear for a loved one's well-being attempted to intrude. What had changed recently? What could be a reason for what was happening?

One thing stood out distinctly. There was a constant factor in the recent changes – their location. They were moving away from Gera. Mik didn't care about the specifics – whether it was a change in latitude, alterations in the magnetic field, fluctuations in pressure or radiation. He was certain that just moments ago, Vist was perfectly fine, and during those brief minutes, they were constantly travelling south-west at a speed of 110 kilometres per hour. Mik rushed to the controls, instructing the autopilot to reverse their course.

After a few minutes, the podvodlod surfaced a considerable distance from the occurrence location, and all reporting systems indicated no abnormalities in the environment, neither in the water nor the air.

Mik sat before Vist, seeing no change in the loader's condition. The green eyes blinked, yet they conveyed no thought. Vist's head turned in response to Mik's calls, and some water at Vist's lips, when offered, was obediently consumed. Mik took Vist by the hand, guided them to their feet and led them to the top deck.

The view here differed greatly from the views of the coastal waters near Gera. Vitr loomed higher in the sky and could easily have been mistaken for Earth's sun if not for its colour and size. The sky here was no longer a deep amethyst but almost blue, with an unpleasant greenish tint. The air and water were hot, and the wind did not cool the travellers' faces. Mik didn't know what else to do. He was already considering whether he should turn home and take his beloved to the cool forests of Terrenia. Still, he noticed that Vist's gaze had become more meaningful and was now looking intensely in one direction. Mik looked back, following this stare, and saw the dark shapes of rocky islands several kilometres away. Mik mused that there might be nothing useful on the islands except shade. While their vessel had plenty of air, fresh water, food and cooling equipment, waiting any longer seemed preferable without aimless drifting. Mik led Vist back inside and took a course towards the islands.

3 Part 3. *Skippers* the Avion

Dr Zina McLeod brought a hot drink to the avion pilot, a slender young woman with sleek black hair. Groonya's skin, a golden brown, was glowing from the inside in places with special implants – on the left side of the neck and both temples. She reclined in a chair, her new spine snug against the back, while her arms relaxed on the armrests. Only her right hand remained encased in a large control glove for urgent commands. Groonya opened her mesmerising eyes and smiled gratefully at Zina. After a brief exchange about her well-being, the girl closed her eyelids again and frowned. The habit of furrowing her brow while piloting the avion was something the young woman inherited from her father, Rodion Baker. Although not a pilot himself, he had to navigate all his creations occasionally, from six-seater tetrahoders to spaceships. Yet, during these endeavours, his once-black eyebrows would furrow down to the bridge of his nose, much like his daughter's now.

Zina glanced at the sea of yellowish clouds beyond the dense transparent polymer and returned to the common area.

Two men were sitting on the round sofa in a round room. They were about the same age but looked like father and son on Earth long ago. Steven McLeod became a loader before decades of life took their toll on his appearance. Although his much-thinning mop of straw-coloured hair had been touched by grey, his face was still relatively smooth and his body strong. On the other hand, Rod Baker opted for all the operations and uploading much later when he had already aged greatly. The alterations did not rejuvenate his looks, but his health and strength were now nearly indistinguishable from other loaders. His mind regained its sharpness, and his former energy and agility returned. His British sense of humour, too.

Both turned as Zina entered, joining them at the low coffee table attached to the floor, a fixture in the avion where everything was secured to the floor and walls. Steven, as always, greeted her with a face beaming with love, and Rod grumbled, "I felt a slight hesitation in the avion during the last manoeuvre. It will take years before she becomes one with the vessel."

"Rod, stop it. Groonya is doing great. Soon she needs to stop for a break one more time and we will reach our destination in less than seven hours after that."

"If Nat was here, we wouldn't need those stops." Steven placed the empty coffee cup on the table, extending his hand to Zina like a thirsty traveller reaching out for a water stream. "He and Groonya would have alternated every six hours, and we'd already be there."

"Every eight, Steve." Zina took his hand, intertwining her fingers with his. "Don't forget, they're both loaders now, and all Nat's skills and experience were added into Groonya's neuroware. She'll get used to them in no time."

Steven turned to Master Baker. "Rod, I know you're the captain on this trip, but why don't you fly — "

With Steven's words, the floor tilted, plates and cups skidding across the table and falling to the floor. Out of habit, Steven moved as if to assist his comrades, but it wasn't necessary. They all hurried to Groonya, whose silence conveyed more concern than any sign of *Skippers* falling.

Lean and swift, Rod was the first to reach his daughter.

Zina followed, hearing his words as she approached.

"What's the matter?" he shouted, but Groonya looked at him with her brown eyes full of panic. Without waiting for an answer, he grabbed her hand, fingers tracing the numerous buttons and touchscreens on the control glove from her wrist to her elbow.

The avion responded by switching to an emergency autopilot and levelling off. Zina and Steven breathed a sigh of relief.

Now Groonya's eyes weren't filled with horror but tears. Finally, she managed to speak, "Father, forgive me . . . I am sorry . . . Captain!"

Rod also calmed down. "It's okay, my girl. What happened? I don't see any problems within the system. Was it a glitch?"

"I don't know. At some point, I felt very strange," Groonya said, bringing the fingers of her left hand to her eyes and studying them. I took the coffee cup and . . . stopped feeling my body. It was as if I had no arms or legs . . ."

Zina bent down to pick up a cup from the wet floor. "Rod, can you land *Skippers*? I need to examine Groonya. This is unprecedented. If it's a glitch, then I don't recognise it."

"Doctor Zina, I feel fine."

"No, Groonya, I'm glad you do, but it doesn't mean something like this won't happen again. I need to know the reason."

Half an hour later, *Skippers* smoothly descended onto a black, shapeless rock sticking out of the water in the company of similar but smaller ones. Several powerful limbs, resembling an insect's segmented legs, grabbed the granite, and the avion froze.

In the medical examination room, equipped for expeditions, Zina sat Groonya under the diagnostic arch and began testing every contact of her implants. Once upon a time, Zina was the chief physician at the University Hospital in New Tokyo, where the second resettlement of earthlings had the most population. But she left that beautiful place and moved to the Altyn district of the white-walled capital, where Steven built a new house for both of them with a laboratory and a private clinic exclusively for loaders. Vist could build loaders, but only Zina and her small team treated, repaired and maintained those full of implants and wires. Loaders rarely needed treatment, with accidents usually befalling Steven, who, due to his incredible bravery, found himself in trouble more often than others.

Zina looked at the readings from Groonya's spinal cord in surprise, unable to discern why she had a blackout.

"But this wasn't a fainting. You said you continued to see the image on the screens."

"Yes, although it was a little rippling."

"I don't understand. It seems your central nervous system lost contact with the neuroware briefly. Maybe you're just overtired. Our stops alone aren't enough. We've been flying for three days now."

"I didn't sleep well during the last landing."

"But you didn't think to tell me? Groonya! We agreed!"

"Sorry, Doctor Zina."

"Okay. We're alive, and everything is fine with *Skippers*. Go to sleep. It's an order. This will help." And Zina pressed a thin, coin-sized disk against the girl's forearm for a second.

***

Groonya slept for fourteen hours, an unusual duration considering that loaders typically require only three or four hours to reset and recharge completely. Steven observed Zina's increasing concerns with each passing hour. Unable to rest, she tossed and turned, finally abandoning the attempt and rising. For the first time, Steven felt relief that she was gone from their bed, letting him drift off. But that did not do him any good either. Although he rarely dreamed and had no sense of how long he had been asleep, he experienced this time a nightmare like never before.

He first dreamed of Vist. Instead of the usual robe, the loader wore the uniform of a field scout, and the width of their shoulders and powerful neck showed him to be a strong man. Vist walked next to Steven in thick green fog, and both shouted the name of Captain Darkwood. They called him several times, and when Steven stopped and listened, it turned out that Vist was no longer by his side. He heard a scream from the fog behind, but it was a woman's scream. Steven ran back and saw green grass under his feet like on Earth. He found a woman lying on her back in the grass with a huge stomach. It was also Vist, but in the throes of childbirth. Steven panicked. He looked around, trying to decide where they were. He saw nothing but fog, full of green dust or pollen floating in the air, like plankton in the sea. When he returned to the woman, it was no longer Vist, but Zina, with a flat stomach and not with her hair cut short for the trip, but with the thick black braid she had on the day they met many years ago. She looked at him with tear-filled eyes and screamed in pain. He realised she was not a loader any longer but an unaltered human, hurting not from contractions but from the loss of all her implants. His beloved Zina was in agony, both from unearthly conditions and from the long years she had lived on Noverca. Before his eyes, her hair turned white, and her face became covered with wrinkles and burns. The grass on the ground withered and disappeared, leaving a reddish crust of cracked clay, and instead of Zina, there lay something that hardly even resembled the remains of a person. But the scream continued to ring in the air. Steven reached out to touch what was left of

Zina but did not recognise his hands. Instead, he had prosthetics that melted, exposing wires and titanium joints.

Steven woke up. His first thought was that the scream he heard was not a dream.

***

Steven woke up completely when he heard the chilling scream again. It was a woman's cry. He hurried to the medical room and saw Groonya screaming. Her eyes were tightly closed; she tried to wave her arms and kick her legs, and Zina attempted to hold her down.

Steven did not ask questions and rushed to help. He grabbed the girl's arms and held both wrists in his large hand. With his other hand, he pinned her thighs to the bed. Zina took advantage of this to inject Groonya with a dose of sedative made from goon-fly venom. Groonya stopped screaming and thrashing a minute later and started breathing evenly. The muscles in her face relaxed, and her eyelids lifted slightly. She slowly said: "Papa . . . pa . . ." and fell asleep.

Zina and Steven stood silently and looked at the girl. Finally, Zina said, "She's never had a nightmare before. Not even as a child. At least that's what she wrote down on her medical form."

"Me neither," Steven said, "I never had bad dreams."

"Why are we talking about you now?"

Steven told Zina about his recent nightmare.

"Interesting." Zina looked at him. "Maybe you heard Groonya's scream in your sleep, and this triggered the dream?"

"Zina, you were sleeping by my side for almost ten years. Has any noise ever woken me up? Even your stupid white bird, which screams every two hours as if being slaughtered, didn't provoke anything except ringing in my ears."

"I must say . . . I could not sleep because I saw Tom's face every time I closed my eyes. But it is not . . . his face. It was too old, as if he was a hundred or something." Zina sighed and stepped towards the door. "What am I talking about? He *is* a hundred and something. I'll go and check on Rodion."

Steven followed Zina, and with every step, his anxiety grew. His vision of Vist was unusual and strangely vivid. In his dream, he even smelled honey wax and dry grass. This bothered him even more than Groonya's experience with her flight earlier.

Rod was out of bed, too. He sat and tinkered with the control chair, trying to find the problems that led to losing its connection with the pilot. His artificial inner ears were switched off so he could not hear but only feel the avion's engines, as a pilot should. Zina shook her head, put her two fingers on Rod's neck, restored his hearing and spoke in the voice of a disappointed nurse.

"Rod, you haven't rested since yesterday. What are you doing to me? I have enough to worry about as it is."

"I rested." Rod answered without even turning around.

"For how many hours?"

"**One.** An' trust me, Zin. That's bleedin' plenty for me."

"Who are you telling all this to? Me?" Zina gasped in indignation.

Steven asked directly, "Rod, have you happened to have any nightmares since we landed?"

Rod stopped fiddling with the pilot's seat and turned around. Steven saw fear on his face that he hadn't seen in years.

"Why did you ask? Are you making a joke?"

"No, neither I, Zina nor Groonya managed to recharge this time. We all had to fight unpleasant dreams. Groonya even screamed, but you didn't hear."

Rod rose to his feet. "I didn't dream nothin'," he said. "I just heard Vist's voice in my ears a few times. At first, I thought it was coming to my implants via satellite, but we left the communication with the O-zont web area long ago. This is why I decided to go deaf and use the chance to run some more tests," Rod said, swinging his arm towards the chair. "But it didn't work. I heard it again just a few minutes ago."

Zina looked at him with wide eyes, "Vist's voice?"

"Let me guess, Vist screamed as if in labour." Steven crossed his arms over his chest.

"No." Rod raised his index finger and tapped his left temple. "Every now and then, I hear one single word right here. *Unload. Unload.* I even thought I was malfunctioning, too."

"Why didn't you tell me?" Zina frowned even more.

"I ain't in the habit of breakin' into someone else's bedroom in the middle of the sleep time."

"Come here." Zina raised both hands and held Rod's head. After a minute, she said, "I can't find anything unusual. But to continue the flight, we must rest before Groonya wakes up. I'll stay with her, and if you, boys, want some sleeping pills—"

"I won't let you out of my sight," Steven said, interrupting her.

"I'll stay with Groonya." Rod started towards the doorway.

Zina sighed. "Okay then. We all shall take a nap in the medical room."

They returned to Groonya, who was sleeping, but her face was tense, and her eyes were darting restlessly under her eyelids.

"Something is wrong with us," Zina said, "Maybe we should stay connected just in case."

Zina settled onto the soft floor, resting against the padded wall, and intertwined her fingers with Rod's, who sat beside her. On the opposite side, Steven stretched out, placing his head on Zina's lap. Tenderly, he grasped her other hand, kissed it and pressed it against his chest. With closed eyes, he pondered the significance of the word "Unload" that Rod had been hearing. What if Vist could indeed be communicating somehow? Recollections of his dream surfaced, where he thought he heard the same word amid the screams of Vist and Zina. Or perhaps it was Groonya's . . . no, that would have been noticed earlier.

Amid the quiet, Steven felt himself slipping away. He could hear Rod's soft snoring and soon found himself transported back to the seashores of Noverca. Desperately, he tried to run, but his feet became ensnared in the treacherous coastal mud while heavy stones cascaded around him, sending up dark, weighty splashes. This mud seemed more like adhesive than ordinary silt. Ahead, he glimpsed the figure of his friend Mik, running effortlessly. They had both been pursued by a horde of frenzied, wild men known as svolochs, and Steven knew that at any moment, one of these stones would crush his skull. He struggled onto the sandy shore, but running didn't become easier. The scout boots on his feet felt as heavy as cannonballs. Behind him, the snarling and snorting of the svolochs drew nearer, threatening to overtake him at any moment.

Suddenly, through this loud and indistinct hum, he heard a clear voice with a metallic undertone saying calmly, "Unload! Steven, unload." He looked up. Mik, still running, turned around and shouted, too, in the voice of Vist, "Unload!"

Steven – not the one who was dreaming, but the one running away from the danger – understood this in his own way. He focused on his shoes, and they released the grip on his feet. Steven kicked off both boots one after the other. The strange and unexpectedly overwhelming lightness from this took his breath away. It seemed to him that he was about to take off into the sky like an avion. He woke up.

Zina sat upright, her breaths coming in rapid gasps, tears streaking down her cheeks. Rod sprang to his feet, shaking his arms like he had just put down two heavy suitcases. Groonya groaned, her hands flailing above the bed as if warding off unseen forces. Steven sat up, enveloping his wife in a tight embrace, pressing her head against his chest, where his own heart was still racing.

It took a few minutes for everyone to return fully to their senses and exchange descriptions of new and unsettling sensations.

Almost like Steven, Zina revisited a terrible moment in her life that happened many years ago on Earth when, before her eyes, mystics called cruisers tortured a friend to death. A cruel man in a sky-blue monk's robe stubbed Chang in the face and shouted, "Ease your soul, free yourself from sin, repent!" The worst thing was that his voice had a metallic undertone.

Rod dreamed he was carrying the broken body of his beloved in his arms. He suffered from the thought that he was about to lose Tolyan and tried to bring him to the temporary system preserver as quickly as possible. He was out of breath and did not have enough strength, and his hands weakened with every second. Suddenly, Tolyan opened his eyes and spoke to him without the usual Russian accent, saying, "Leave me and take care of our children." Rod saw that it was not Tolyan but Obydva and lowered him onto the reddish sand of the Western Bay near the white-walled capital.

Groonya could not say anything in detail. She sobbed and said that one of her fathers untied her bound hands and, instead of saving himself, sacrificed his life for her, and she could not even tell which one of them she saw in her dream. Perhaps she didn't know.

"Do we have a blue salt totem on board?" Steven asked after the pause.

"Nah, Marchel's decognitivator wouldn't work while you're sleeping, and none of us has a headache." Rod shook his head slowly, "But these dreams are unnatural and provoked by somethin' else."

All four sat at the low coffee table in the common room, all feeling rather uneasy.

Zina said confidently, "We did not dream. Too early into sleep. It's the wrong stage for such brain activity, wrong … well, everything. And too much in common. The images are different and must be a product of our memories and fears. But unlike dreams, they all carry the same message."

Groonya looked at Zina with huge eyes enhanced by altered irises. "Someone is trying to communicate, using our dreams."

"Using them? More like violating them," Steven added.

"And it only works when we are not quite conscious," Zina said, finishing this chain of thoughts. "Although it is trying even when we are. Rod said he heard the voice when he was awake, too."

"Not quite awake." Rod grumbled, "When I work, I occasionally get into an automated state and lose sense of time."

"Fine, but in every dream, two things stand out and connect them all." Zina looked at everyone in turn, saying, "The message is trying to rid us of something and appears to be coming from Vist, although not directly."

"Unload, drop, leave, free . . . I don't get it!" Steven put both fists on his knees. "What does Vist want us to do?"

"We are all loaders," Groonya said in a quiet voice.

"Unload? Vist wants us to . . . unload?" Steven turned to his wife, "Is it possible? And why? Can you remove implants? What would it do to us?"

"We cannot remove them." Zina looked at Rodion Baker. "Rod, you might die. And the rest will not react to it well either. Also, I don't think we should understand it so literally."

"I wanna know why Vist tried to instruct us if she did and how she managed to do it. We're out of web coverage." Rod threw his hands up with his fingers outstretched.

"Right. But we may be within reach of Vist."

Everyone looked at Groonya. Rod's face relaxed, showing full attention, "What are you saying, my girl?"

"Dad, Captain . . . what I felt on the bed and on that chair were very different. The dream was strange, and I felt watched, and there was an expectation of some sort. But during the flight, I was cut off from all my senses. I could not feel the avion and my whole body because I *was* an avion then."

Zina put her hand over Groonya's cold fingers, "Do not worry too much. I will not draw any conclusions now, but we should decide what to do next. I want to fully examine us all, but we must leave these rocks soon. We cannot stay here for more than a cycle."

"I am afraid to get on that chair again," Groonya said, looking devastated.

"You don't 'ave to, my girl," Rod said, "You and I will fly the avion manually, and we will do it together."

***

"I'm afraid Rod won't be able to take us home. Groonya, this burden might fall on your shoulders," Zina said, her tone sombre as the danger passed and Captain Baker's face relaxed.

Coming out of stasis was tough, and they almost lost him.

"Yes, our captain has completely given up lately. He's an old wreck. I told him many times —"

Steven's words were interrupted by a raspy voice. "You are a wreck, Stevie-boy. You spent more time in a hospital bed than all of us put together," Rod said, opening his eyes and turning to Groonya. "You can handle it, my girl. I know."

Groonya was no longer crying. Though her face remained flushed and her eyes swollen, she breathed steadily, her attention fixed on her father. She nodded with determination. "I can handle it. Doctor Zina found a way to avoid any major surgery."

Rod's gaze shifted to Zina, who said, "There was no need to remove the implants. I simply severed contact between *Skipper*'s senses and Groonya's central nervous system."

Rod's eyes widened. "What? Zina, you're not going to turn around now. Our mission has not been completed. I am the captain, and my orders are—"

"Rod, my friend, you are now only the captain of *Skipper*, and you both will be lying flat for . . . only O'Teka knows how long," Steven interrupted him this time. "I took command of the expedition. If Zina and I had decided to quit, we would be back home already."

"We now have a speedboat with a small ZPE engine," Groonya added, "and we are sitting in the middle of a chain of islands that stretches in the right direction. I will see if I can get to the mainland on our boat. It's not that far away."

Rod was surprised. "Where did we get the speedboat?"

"I built it," Steven replied. "I had to take some things off *Skipper* to make my *Cutter*, but I promise to return everything. Groonya was a great help."

Rod was even more surprised. "How long ago did we land?"

"We've been sitting on the island for almost a month."

"But you let Timofey know?" Rod asked.

Steven scratched his ear. "Uh, no. I needed to dismantle both our 'postmen.' Their small reactors had to be removed."

"Both of them?"

"One was sufficient for me, but the second came in handy too. Zina didn't sit idle either during that time. Tell him, Zin."

"While you were in stasis and Steven worked on his *Cutter*, Groonya and I reprogrammed the messenger, connected it to a portable diagnostic device, and sent it in a spiral around our island. Each new circle added several miles to the diameter and some readings from the area, including the region where Groonya lost control in the air on the way here."

Rod pondered for a moment before speaking. "Okay, I am ready to ask about my health."

Zina smiled a little, "You took your time. Steven is right; you're not in the best shape now. When we entered that zone – let's call it that – your age caught up with you. You were uploaded so late in life that Vist had to add many new implants to restore your health. Now, your regenerated tissues are ageing rapidly. Since we're currently out of the zone and your artificial system is working again, you've still lost a lot and should avoid going back there. *Skippers* is the safest place for you now. You must stay here or go home. We all knew what you would choose, so I'll do my best to keep you alive here until we have something to report back to O'Teka and the colony."

"Groonya and I will ensure we find some answers, I promise," Steven added.

Rod closed his eyes. "Steven, do not give a promise that you might not be able to keep. Not everything depends on you."

"I know. I just promise to do my best. Remember, we will cease being loaders once we go to the zone."

"That's why the first trip on the *Cutter* is mine," Groonya asserted, "as I am the youngest crew member. I'm not artificially regenerating yet and should not be affected. I'll be the pioneer in exploring what lies ahead from here. Yes, Dad. Dr Zina cannot be wrong, and she will also help me name all those new islands."

***

Groonya's first expedition began with an unusually clear sky overhead. As the radiant star Vitricus bestowed its golden caress upon the tranquil waters, Groonya navigated the petite vessel crafted by Steven towards the beckoning line of the first island. With a grumpy murmur, the ZPE engine propelled her forwards.

In Groonya's mind, she fancied herself a character plucked from the pages of an adventurous tome – a seeker of treasures and revealer of clandestine enigmas. She stood tall at the control panel, and her raven-black hair flowed in the wind behind her. She could see only with one eye since her artificial eyeball doubled as a camera but no longer interfaced with her nervous system. Groonya thought if she were a little younger, she would probably decorate herself with a stylish eye patch to add to the game.

As the boat, christened *Cutter*, gently nudged the sandy shoreline, Groonya's excitement reached its zenith. She grasped her radio, then connected back to the avion with her report, "Behold, I dub this land 'Pancake.' 'Tis as flat as a well-flipped flapjack and adorned with sands of a reddish hue, sparkling with mica or quartz. I spy a handful of pebbles and . . . ah, yes! A congregation of rock snails, ready to sate a wanderer's hunger!"

Steven's voice crackled from the ether. "It's a charming idea, but can you check the meter and tell me how far it is from us?"

"Hmm . . . approximately 5.4 kilometres, Master. There is no foliage in sight and I see a single fish bone. At least, I think it was a fish. I shall embark on a reconnaissance to seek signs of human presence."

"Very well, but remember to check in every twenty minutes and keep your settings on."

"I know the drill, Master McLeod. We tinkered with radios like this back in school. You copied a relic from Earth's yesteryears, but with a much longer range. This is what humans used before the amulets, right?"

"Even before cuff phones. But I've added a failsafe. Any sudden noise triggers it."

"Understood. Should a pirate cross my path, I'll scream as loud as I can," said Groonya, chuckling then signing off.

Groonya walked around the island with the radio snug in her breast pocket and found nothing. Yet, upon her return to *Cutter*, a peculiar splash caught her ear, distinct from the serf's rhythmic lull. Intrigued, she scanned the waves green with plankton, seeing only drifting seaweed strands.

The next isle, a mere stone's throw away, assumed a rounder, loftier form, earning the moniker Donut. Then, Groonya charted her course southwards, christening the subsequent landmasses Toast, Scone and Cram, reserving special scrutiny for the largest – Loaf.

"Master, I see a peculiar marking on the sand – a trace of some aquatic behemoth's dalliance with terra firma. Might I have an unseen escort?" Groonya asked, a hint of worry in her voice.

"I can't tell, but if you do, your tail better be a fast swimmer like *Cutter*. Doubt it. Keep your eyes peeled; some critters can stroll on land."

"True. These marks don't scream agility. I reckon I can outpace it," Groonya mused confidently.

"Don't get cocky, Groonya. Initial impressions can deceive. Snap a photograph of those marks for documentation," Steven advised. "Do you know what an Earth marine animal, a seal, looked like?"

"Nope."

On Loaf, fortune smiled on Groonya at last. Amid her thorough examination, she stumbled upon a relic – a firepit, its embers long extinguished.

"Master, I've found the remnants of a campfire – ancient yet inimitable human in origin. I have no idea what was burned here. There is not much vegetation. A sparse tuft of dry grass can be a kindling, yet little else. These ashes do not give me any clue."

"Very well. Permit me to consult my esteemed assistant." Steven's voice was momentarily replaced by a velvety voice with a hint of a French accent.

"Bonjour, Groonya. Would you take a sample of those ashes for me? You should have sterile containers in your kit."

"Of course, Doctor Zina. Anything else?"

"Indeed. Search for a ... vessel – a receptacle for water, perhaps."

Soon, Groonya called again: "I almost overlooked it, but behold – a rock snail shell, hollowed and blackened with soot."

"Marvellous!" said Steven. "In these latitudes, you don't need fire for warmth. Tom made himself a snail soup!"

"Or," said Dr Zina, "perhaps it served a more utilitarian purpose – boiled potable water, wound cleansing, blade sterilisation."

"I'd rather not ponder," muttered Groonya, a shiver coursing through her.

As if on cue, a splash echoed from the vicinity of the old camp. Groonya sprang to her feet and perched on a waterlogged boulder. Her good eye fixed on the pale figure swaying with the waves beneath the surface – a mesmerising and unnerving spectacle. With bated breath, she leaned over the boulder's edge, her heart a tumultuous drumbeat.

Beneath the emerald water's surface, three large eyes fixated on the young woman.

"Hey boss, Doc, I'm staring at the biggest blobster ever," Groonya said. "It's like a large man – a massive one! I saw similar forms in the temple paintings at that Japanese museum exhibit, but this one's got tentacles."

"Better get back, Groonya," Dr Zina advised.

"You in trouble?" Steven asked.

"Nah, not yet," Groonya replied, waving casually to the creature.

To her surprise, the underwater giant emerged, its curvy form shimmering in Vitr's light. Its three intelligent eyes possibly conveyed a mix of curiosity and concern. Still, Groonya blamed her imagination for that and backed away to the campfire, observing from afar as the blobster awkwardly manoeuvred onto the sandy shore, its movements resembling a heavy, clumsy walk.

Paused and dripping, the creature visibly struggled on land. It stood on three very fat tentacles pressed together, supporting its mass like one broad column.

Groonya lifted both hands in front of her, gesturing for the creature to stop its advance. "Easy, buddy. No need to venture too far from your habitat, although you could use a bit of a suntan," she remarked.

Suddenly, the blobster extended two upper limbs, each adorned with a knot of tiny tentacles. Five of those stuck out, imitating human fingers.

"I hope you're snapping pictures of that," Steven said when Groonya described the scene.

"I am, I am . . ." Groonya exclaimed. "I think it's trying to communicate. I've never heard of an intelligent blobster before. Have you, Doctor Zina?"

"No, but this planet never ceases to surprise me. Could it have encountered a human before?" Zina pondered.

"I doubt it. It's just mimicking my movements and . . . wow! Doctor Zina, you might be onto something," Groonya said.

"Why?" Steven asked.

"Because it just gave me the thumbs up with both hands. If I can call them that," Groonya replied.

"O'Teka!" Zina said, "Tom used to do that . . . with both hands!"

"It's true," Steven added. "Groonya, can you move your hand as if you were tearing a necklace off your chest and throwing it to the side? Groonya? Hey ... Groonya! What's happening? What's all that splashing?"

But Groonya couldn't answer; she couldn't scream as she was submerged, her radio lying on the sand beside the cold firepit.

***

Groonya breathed. This time, slow, deep inhalations and even longer exhalations were beyond her control. Something else was dictating the rhythm of her breathing. The world seemed to pause around her, with only the pulse of the ocean's waves pushing and pulling against her.

Once the initial shock subsided and her panic ebbed away, Groonya found herself in a state of suspended animation. It was as though the situation itself awaited her analysis and evaluation. She ceased struggling and remained still, enveloped in numerous tentacles' firm-yet-painless embrace.

Underwater, her captor resembled a blobster more than it did on land – a balloon on a string, but upside down. A long tentacle extended from the cluster of its limbs, reaching upward to the surface. It likely served as an umbilical cord for air, providing for Groonya and possibly itself.

Her good eye, wide open, struggled to pierce the murky depths of the ocean water. Looking upwards, she could barely discern the shimmering dance of the mercury-like surface just metres above her head. The slanting rays of Vitr danced among the plankton. Three bottomless eyes loomed in front of her face, seemingly observing her with expectation.

Groonya recalled how this creature, resembling a fat and clumsy man on the surface, had almost been given a name by her when, suddenly, its upper limbs wrapped around her head in a cold and slippery knot. Her mouth was covered, and in an attempt to break free, she dropped her gear.

The next moment, the Jellykid – yes, she decided to call it that – dragged her beneath the malachite waves and held her there, doing nothing else but pumping breathable air through the flat tentacle around Groonya's jaw.

Her hands were free, and she felt other tentacles encircle her ribcage, holding her in place while also controlling or monitoring her breathing.

Jellykid held her before its eyes like a human child holding a doll, perhaps observing with fascination the movements of her long black hair swirling around her head.

Recalling how the creature had attempted to communicate using the Ikhtees sign language on the shore, Groonya wondered if she could do the same underwater.

Maybe her arms were free for that very purpose. It made sense, she thought, lifting her fingers and trying to recall the appropriate words. What should she ask? Starting with a single word, she said, "Why?"

Jellykid lifted its limb with five extended tentacles or fingers . . .

Groonya again used Dr Zina's naming skill and dubbed the creature's appendages "fintacles." Those fintacles formed an unmistakeable "Okay" in front of her face.

Okay, thought Groonya. What are you up to then? She signed the word "boat" in Ikhtees. In response, Jellykid's three eyes turned to the left and up, possibly indicating the direction of the dark shape on the surface. Groonya guessed correctly; it was the bottom of her *Cutter*.

"Tom," she signed, and for the first time, the creature jerked and started to sign something indecipherable. Looks like you know the language better than I do, Groonya thought, lifting both hands to cover her eyes for a second – a sign of not understanding in Ikhtees. But Jellykid seemed to grasp her confusion and stopped, staring at her.

Groonya tried again, this time with two words, "Why water?"

"No noise," answered Jellykid.

"Yeah, I guess we were rather noisy up there with all that radio and shouting," Groonya thought.

"You know Tom?" she signed with her fingers.

"Yes."

"Where—" Groonya started, but Jellykid, with its lower tentacles, propelled towards the dark shadow at the surface. In a flash, the creature gently lifted Groonya above the surface and lowered her into the boat, removing the ribbon-like tentacle from her lips.

Looking around, Groonya noticed that the land she called Loaf was several metres away and quickly getting further from her. She realised that Jellykid had started to pull or push *Cutter* away at a considerable speed. Deciding not to resist this opportunity, she refrained from interfering with her engine. She just wished that the radio was still with her. But Groonya still had her boat, meaning she could return for it.

***

Groonya had been missing for almost a year. Initially, Steven and Zina only knew that she had encountered a creature resembling a blobster, but one that could speak a few words in the Silent Tongue of the Ikhtees.

A couple of cycles after the young woman mysteriously disappeared, Steven hastily constructed something like a raft with a sail and a small motor using the last field ZPE-converters, depriving the expedition of the opportunity to inform the colony about their situation.

He and Zina followed Groonya's path to the island where she had discovered the remains of a bivouac. Zina insisted on staying on the island and waiting for either Groonya or the blobster to shed light on what had happened. As the only yachtsman, Steven was forced to return to the avion to look after old Rod, whose health had seriously deteriorated after the "unloading." Rod moved with great difficulty, was almost deaf, and at times fell into episodes of expressing an aggressive desire to act or complete oblivion. He often forgot to eat and maintain his hygiene, so Steven had to become his nurse.

On the fourth cycle, Zina reported encountering a blobster whose vocabulary in the Ikhtees language was limited. However, it knew Groonya's name and the word "safe." Steven promptly joined Zina on the island, only to find out that the blobster refused to show the girl's location with a cryptic explanation that meant, in simple words: "She is alone, and there are already two of you." Zina had already tried several words that the blobster did not understand at all, such as "child," "parent," "friend" and "family." However, it understood the words "home" and "worry," as well as the concept of a message.

On the fifth cycle, the blobster brought Zina what she had hoped for – a large, flat piece of fishbone with several lines written in

Groonya's hand. This convinced Zina that Rod's daughter was not in immediate danger and was busy collecting useful information. Zina persuaded the blobster to pass her a radio. Soon, communication was established between the avion and the cave, although it was not entirely reliable. Groonya explained why *Skippers* should not approach the mainland and that they just needed to take care of her father and wait. No one knew then how long they would have to do that. But finally, Groonya was returned to them, and they were all together again.

"Well, we're all glad you're finally back with us," Steven said, finishing the story.

Groonya turned her eyes from his heavily tanned face and bald head to the visibly aged face of Doctor Zina. Master McLeod and his wife now resembled those once-especially healthy and athletic people on Earth who had reached their sixties or older. Not a single black hair was left in the woman's grown-out curls. They were white as milk, and wrinkles spread out from the corners of Steven's eyes, making his face seem even more smiley. Both lost weight, but because these changes happened in just a few months, Groonya was amazed at the difference. However, they still looked strong and beautiful. The same could not be said about her father, whom Dr Zina had just put into an induced coma at the temporary system preserver in an attempt to prolong his life. Under the transparent dome, he resembled a mummy more than a living person. Rodion Baker could die.

"Groonya, I beg you, stop blaming yourself," said Zina. "Of course, we were very worried when you disappeared, but when Steven built the raft, and we met your Jellykid, even your father calmed down a little. Unfortunately, his mind started to wander, returning him to events long past. He once tried to assure me that we had not yet left the colony and once that we were still on Earth. This time, he has decided that this was the cycle when you disappeared. He got anxious, manually lifting *Skippers* while we were ... sleeping, and flew into the zone."

"We didn't understand right away what was happening," said Steven, "and he was already circling over a large rock with the letter *G* painted on it. He landed on the rock and even managed to get out. It was too late to stop him. Fortunately, the blobsters quickly realised he had come for you, but it was up to me to fly *Skippers* back. Yes ... I had to learn how while waiting."

Groonya remembered how she felt when the old man threw his arms around her and collapsed as if he had died, and she started sobbing again.

"It's okay; don't worry about me. I wish I knew ... We need to take Father to your hospital so you can fix him," she said to Zina, who took her hand. Then she turned to Steven, "Now we must return to Gera. Master, you and I can take turns flying."

"Until I am happy with your health, you will not fly anything, Groonya." Zina's voice was still sympathetic but firm. "You lived in a damp cave, eating I don't know what, and drinking salty water. I need to check your filters and ... well ... everything."

"And you need to tell me about Tom, the monster the blobsters warned you about and what happened to my *Cutter*. It may be worth it for me to check other areas."

"No, it's not safe, and not because of the monster. Master, you might not come back from such a trip. You will age and die within a cycle or two. Here you two were just fishing occasionally, and look at you now . . . We need to leave these parts as soon as possible. We will come back to find Tom. We need younger people only . . . no implants, no loader technology or computers . . . simple equipment only . . ."

Groonya was almost shouting but had to stop, coughing and breathing heavily.

"Enough," said Zina. "Come with me. Rod is stable for now, so let's decide what to do next when you are better."

But it was too early for *Skippers* to go home. A few cycles later, when Groonya's condition became satisfactory from Zina's point of view, and the avion was serviced and ready to fly from Steven's point of view, the young woman left *Skippers* and went to the sea to swim in the hot water one last time.

She took off her shirt but immediately pressed it to her chest because an unfamiliar young voice called out to her from the shadows of the coastal rocks.

"If you are not Groonya Baker, then I will believe that fairy nymphs live in these parts."

Groonya turned her good eye towards the rocks and saw a young man with long black hair and narrow eyes sitting in the shade. He smiled without a hint of embarrassment. He was wet as if he had just come out of the water fully dressed, although his top was wrapped around his neck like a scarf. His protective goggles were pushed to the top of his head, and his pants looked rather too weathered for ucha-silk.

Groonya turned away, put on her shirt and walked up to him with quick steps.

"Who are you?" she asked, "Has the colony sent a new rescue expedition for the commander and architexter?"

"And for you, too. I see that half the work has already been done. All that remains is to find *Marlin* and its crew and return home triumphantly. My name is Naoki, and I was just dragged under the water on some kind of lasso from your cave. I don't know how I stayed alive. Blobsters swim faster than your tiny boat, so we must wait for the Korub couple to catch up with me."

Part 4. Purpose

Obydva brought two cups of tock milkshakes to the table.

"Here we go, guys. Happy holidate, and well done, both of you!"

The two boys had nearly finished their breakfast. One chewed and hummed, though without any particular tune or rhythm. He swung both legs and worked through warmed bread and cheese, which made his pink ears dance.

The other sat still, methodically gathering the last remnants of sour cream and sugar from the plate with half a pancake as if cleaning it. The boy's face frowned with concentration.

Obydva silently observed them both. He had grown accustomed to the boys' differences but occasionally found it unsettling.

"What shall we do?" he asked, gathering the empty plates. "Shall we go crab hunting, or do you have plans?"

Dmitro ceased swinging his legs and turned his eager face to his father.

"I have plans! I want to go to Uncle Mirat's. Bella's birthdate is soon; he'll teach me how to grow fianits. I'll make her a pendant as a gift. And you promised a ball match."

"Excellent plan. But Bella's birthdate is still a way off."

"Papa, crystals take a long time to grow, and I need a perfect one that is rather large."

"Understood. Well, Yar, what would you like to do?" Obydva turned to Yar'oma.

The purple-hued boy set his milkshake on the table and lifted his silver eyes.

"May I go to the temple?" His voice was subdued.

"Really? Don't you want a break from school?"

"Not that. I want to visit the Earth Museum."

"We visited there a few weekends ago."

"Yes, but I didn't . . . see everything."

Obydva carefully replayed these words in his head. Of course. The boy meant to say, "I didn't find *something*." He recalled how, during their last visit, while he and Dmitro had spent a good half hour disassembling and reassembling the first model of tetrahoder, Yar'oma had wandered slowly from one rescued escape pod to another.

"I told you, son. The SD-211 isn't there. I . . . Pilot Marta Larsson saw it descending into the Southern Ocean. With her own eyes!"

"You told me that story," the boy said, crestfallen. I want to explore something else."

Obydva smiled at both boys. "All right then. We'll drop Dmitro at Master Mirat's and head to the museum. After that, we'll regroup, have lunch, do some shopping and play ball until you've had your fill. Deal?"

Dmitro nodded, and Yar'oma shrugged.

"Get ready, then, and don't forget your sports shoes."

Obydva exited the kitchen, thinking that he really ought to speak with the history

129

teacher. It seemed Yar was asking questions again.

Thirty minutes later, he sat on a wall bench on the forty-second floor of the Great Temple of O'Teka, home to the Museum of the Second Wave of Migrants from Earth. Many years ago, they had journeyed to Noverca through the Maisers' wormhole in hundreds of small capsules, each the size of an eight-seater conmot. While most capsules had been recycled, a few lost during landing ended up here. Architexter Vist's search party had discovered and rescued them almost two generations ago. Obydva possessed intimate knowledge of each capsule, not through his own memory but through the memories of the two deceased group members from which he was assembled.

Obydva was neither Tolyan nor Marta, yet he somehow managed to embody their finest qualities, principles, affections, characteristics, habits, professionalism and even their Eastern European accent. For instance, he couldn't quite fathom why he felt such a strong bond with Tolyan's husband and children and with Marta's student, Nat Alloyway. Nevertheless, he learned something new about human passion for things seemingly unrelated to oneself. Thus, he observed with great interest the nine-year-old boy, whom everyone regarded as his adopted son and whom he (along with perhaps Vist and Zina) secretly considered his grandson. Biologically, Yar'oma and Obydva weren't linked, yet a direct familial connection existed between what was loaded into Obydva's head and that which was loaded into Yar's mother's head. Because of Obydva's deep care for Yar'oma, he understood the boy's persistent search for information in the museum and historical archives.

The boy was the outcome of a crime, developed in an artificial womb after being removed from the woman's body. The details of this atrocious act, although recorded in the temple, remain inaccessible to most colonists.

Obydva's thoughts were echoed by the words of Architexter Timofey Hesley: "It will be a long time before Yar'oma can pray offerings about his parents in the temple."

The figure in the long white robe settled onto the bench beside the loader. "Never, I hope," Obydva replied without taking his eyes from the boy.

Yar'oma stood near the temporary system preserver model, which was outdated even by Earth standards.

"He will be older and wiser then."

"I sometimes suspect he already knows something. Tim, can you scan him?"

"Even if I could, I wouldn't. You should discuss this with Vist when they return."

"We'll revisit this conversation if they don't. Can you believe Yar asked his biology teacher if people and svolochs can interbreed?"

"Children can be curious. I remember asking my teachers if you could cross blobsters with bulldogs."

"But he also questioned his history teacher about cannibalism on Earth, and the damn machine answered him!"

"I don't understand your concern." Timofey Hesley attempted to take his friend by the hand, but Obydva pulled away.

"I worry he'll start crafting his own family history, filling the gaps with fantasy and whims."

"Obydva, this is highly unlikely and not typical here. Yar is Novercian. We rely on reason, not whims."

"He's not a typical child. And unlikely doesn't mean impossible."

"True." Timofey rose, prepared to depart. "Let me know when *you* have a genuine cause for concern. Have you heard from Nat yet?"

"No. *I do* have a valid reason to worry about Nat."

***

The projected clouds above the white wall turned pink, and the blue sky between them brightened. The colour combination was beautiful, but the pain was too much to look up at. Yar'oma bent down and spat out a bloody mass on the grey slabs. He just couldn't run any more.

He stopped to catch his breath and leaned against the stack of concrete blocks by the eastern city wall. The stitching pain in his right side was unbearable. Still, he was more worried about possible internal bleeding in the kidney area where Round Bob had kicked him repeatedly. However, Yar'oma wasn't just trying to get away from those boys. He was leading them away from his brother. Both minions of Bazza Nobel had started after him with the enthusiasm of trained hounds. Baz would finish Dmitro if the pack's animal instinct did not possess him. He couldn't help himself and ran after Yar'oma, too. Damned earthlings!

The boy with purple skin and silver close-set eyes listened carefully. Nothing. There was no sound of pursuit. Yar'oma may have been fragile, but he was faster, and the boys seemed to have given up the chase.

These fights had gone too far, and he must do something to stop them. But that was a matter for another cycle. First, the boy had to find help. He needed an adult with an amulet – any adult. Yar'oma looked around. He didn't realise he had reached the city's edge, where no one went except ordermen and part-time scouts. What safety could he find here?

He stood up, holding onto the concrete block, but immediately sat down again, groaning in pain. He couldn't go and search for help, and calling out was also dangerous; his pursuers might still be close. If they found him, he would remain there forever. There were no people here at this time of the cycle. He was unable to move on. All that was left was to lie there and hope that he would either rest and recover or get worse, quickly lose consciousness and die.

He became aware of a presence at some indistinct point in his semi-conscious state. It was impossible to tell whether his mind, addled by fever or fatigue, had conjured it from the recesses of his imagination – perhaps a fragment of some primal archetype.

The figure, though fleeting, was vivid. It resembled an old woman, grotesque and weathered, with an uneven purple face. She did not speak but stood over him, her gaze fixed and inscrutable. He was too weak to ask her to help him.

He couldn't tell whether she was real or a product of his delirium. Yet the sensation was visceral as she leaned closer and, with a deliberate motion, tucked something into his pocket. Without a word, she turned and vanished.

If only he had an amulet. But he was underage and lacked sufficient qualifications to possess an amulet or choose a purpose. Although he already had a very good idea of what he wanted to do, he still had six years to wait until adulthood. That was if he lived long enough.

So he lay with his eyes closed and breathed slowly, not knowing he already had an amulet. Or rather, its simplest version, which only Yar'oma's father, Obydva, knew of. As soon as his sons learned to walk, he inserted a small device, the size of a peppercorn, under the boys' shoulder blades, the only function of which was to inform Obydva of their coordinates. This is why, when Yar'oma opened his eyes again, he saw Dmitro's smiling face in the back seat of his father's conmot.

"He's awake!" his brother said loudly over his shoulder and added quietly, "Yar, are you in pain?"

Yar'oma listened to his body. "Not any more."

Dmitro nodded, stopped smiling and leaned closer. "I told you to leave Nobel and Bob to me," he whispered reproachfully. "I'm an earthling, like them. You could probably handle the Minibear alone. Although he is a solid Nordian, he is awfully clumsy."

"Father can hear us; you don't have to whisper," Yar'oma said. "I didn't want Bob to kick you to death. It would be better if I — "

"Are you now our hero and martyr?" Dmitro sat up straight with a frown on his face. "If you were older than me, I would have understood. But we agreed – everything shared equally, even bruises and bumps. They could have caught you and beaten you to the last blood."

"Now it will be more difficult for them to do this," said Obydva, wearily. "Tomorrow, all three are going in for rehabilitation. And if you don't want to join them, you'll tell me everything right now."

The conmot stopped near the Altyn Central Clinic, and Obydva turned his seat one hundred and eighty degrees to be face to face with the boys.

"Doctor Scarlett is waiting for you, Yar, and I will talk to Dmitro while she examines you. But you must start talking first."

The boys looked at each other, and Yar'oma began the story.

A few weeks ago, one of the schoolchildren from the group in which the brothers took wrestling lessons lost first place to Dmitro in the tournament, and he really didn't like it. At first, Baz Nobel behaved like a real

Novercian, even shaking hands with his worthy opponent. But after a few cycles, he and two students from a parallel group challenged Dmitro to a real duel outside the boundaries of the capital's gym. This was against the rules, and when Dmitro refused the rematch, Bazza, Round Bob and Shanil, nicknamed Minibear, began teasing Dmitro as a coward. They didn't manage to spread rumours around the school since ordinary Novercians don't approve of such things. But Bazza Nobel wanted to win a fight too much, even if it wasn't fair.

He had waylaid the brothers on the way home through Paradise Park. Bazza declared loudly that Dmitro was a weakling, his brother was a svoloch, and their whole family were descendants of dubious origin. Dmitro approached the bully to say something to him but was punched in the face. A fight was inevitable. It was short because some passers-by called out to them, and all five ran away from the park because they did not want to be identified.

"But it didn't happen this cycle, did it?" asked Obydva.

"No. Since then, we have fought four times, usually in the early hours, so that the bruises and scratches would have time to heal by sleep time and the parents would not notice anything," replied Yar'oma.

"I see. It's time to go to your appointment. And you" – Father turned to Dmitro – "wait for me here."

***

When Obydva returned alone a few minutes later, he sat silently and stared at his son.

"It's my fault," Dmitro said after a pause. "If that cycle, after the first fight, when we arrived at the square, I hadn't said anything, everyone else would have kept their ideas to themselves."

"I don't understand," said Obydva.

"No one was mad any more; the steam was let out, but I had never felt in the gym what I felt after that fight. Not even during the tournaments or the awards ceremonies."

Obydva looked carefully into Dmitro's eyes. "Describe those feelings."

"I will try. It's . . . as if the air suddenly became sweet. Every cell in my body seemed to tremble, my thoughts were clearer than ever, and . . . I swear . . . I felt the hair on the back of my neck stand on end."

Obydva grinned and asked, "Did you feel like you had become stronger and were ready to fight the whole school?"

"Yes!" Dmitro replied, surprised. "I wanted . . . to take off my shoes and run through the whole city barefoot."

"Even so? Okay, so what happened next?"

"I told Yar about this. We spoke quietly, and he replied that he wanted to take off more than just his shoes and would like to be in the northern valley, where the snow never melts. Our opponents were a hundred metres further, but apparently, Minibear heard us with his hairy ears, and all three came closer. They were no longer aggressive, but Nobel said to come to the salt warehouse in the early hours of the next cycle. They turned around and left. Nobel didn't even wait for an answer; he knew now we would come."

"What's all this talk about the last blood?"

"I'll tell you. After the first proper battle, we washed our wounds in a drainage ditch under the city wall. I felt great. Yar, apparently, too. We violated all wrestling rules in such a way that three of us had broken ribs and fingers. It took two cycles for them to regrow. Do you remember last weekend when I refused to play volleyball? But then, none of us were sorry at all; we even had a laugh. Round Bob suddenly said, 'Do you want to feel even better?' I didn't believe it could be better. And Nobel added, 'If we not only forget about the rules of fighting but also agree to fight to the death, then ... '" Dmitro fell silent and lowered his eyes. "Yar then said no, but I agreed. Nobel was right. This cycle, it was so good to fight that I forgot about the danger for Yar. His wounds heal quicker than mine, but he gets them easier. I only remembered it when I woke up alone and realised that Bob had knocked me out with brass knuckles. Yar led them away so they wouldn't finish me off. I didn't immediately figure out what to do; my head still hurt a lot, but I was worried that they would catch up with him."

Obydva paused and said, "This is not the first time I've heard of such a reaction, but Mik and Steven talked about young scouts and cadets. No one at your age has been registered yet, but I'm afraid a week's rehabilitation for all five cannot be avoided. After it is over, I will train you myself. I haven't forgotten how to do it yet."

"What will happen to us during the rehabilitation?" Dmitro asked.

"Total solitude with time to reflect," Obydva replied. "And O'Teka will remind you why each of us has an animal inside and why *we* have to control it, not the other way around."

The conversation was interrupted by a very short, hypertrichosian woman with a clean-shaven face and a thick mop of red and grey hair. She opened the door to the conmot and let Yar'oma in; his forehead reddened by the diagnosis probes and a medicine-administering device attached to his neck.

"There is no serious tissue damage. The torn vessels are already healing. I gave him something to speed up the process. Let him eat more protein and sleep at least six hours," the short woman said, smiling at Yar'oma instead of saying goodbye.

"Thank you, Scarlett," said Obydva. "I owe you two pork pies and ale on top of the usual payment."

She nodded and left. Only Obydva noticed how much disaffection there actually was in her smile. She didn't like Yar'oma, but for reasons of her own.

***

The three boys who initiated the fight received seven cycles of rehabilitation. Dmitro, who was the target, received six cycles and Yar'oma, who initially refused and fought only to protect his brother, received five. A cycle difference did not seem like much, but the boys found it to be a very long twenty-four hours inside.

Yar'oma was no stranger to solitude. He often chose to be alone and could occupy himself under any circumstances. But this time, he had no access to the archives of O'Teka, and listening to a lecture for one hour per cycle, attending counselling sessions, asking and answering questions, were his only contacts with the external world and the only interactive activities he was allowed to have. The rest of the time, he had to reflect, think, introspect and contemplate. He tried composing poetry in his head, as he had nothing to write on, but he did not like his work this time. His poems sounded flat and meaningless.

The holo-walls had a very limited selection of images, which only added to his loneliness despite their beauty and therapeutic sounds.

During his last cycle, he got up from the bed and went to the bathroom to do his hygiene routine. Then he put on fresh clothing – a perfectly clean white tracksuit – and asked the walls to project a clearing in the black forest. The rays of the low-hanging Vitr made their way through the trunks of trees with dark foliage and illuminated the rare poplar fluff, **slowly falling like snow onto the blue grass**. Yar'oma was tired of looking at the icy desert of permafrost he had chosen initially.

A small screen on the cabinet door showed that breakfast was waiting. Yar'oma found a usual bowl of nutritious but tasteless purée there, ate it and sat on a chair before a large rectangle on the wall. He thought about how this rehabilitation made him reflect not so much on whether he should or should not break the rules and take part in the dangerous game but about the strange feelings he had afterwards.

Yar'oma tried to remember those feelings. Strangely, what had seemed so clear back then was now blurry and foggy. No matter how hard he tried, he couldn't resurrect those sensations. He remembered the desire to do something completely out of character and nothing more.

While waiting, he turned a flat beach pebble he had been carrying with him for some time over and over in his hand. He didn't know where he got it from. On the pebble was written "Find me."

Finally, the screen on the wall came to life. He quickly returned the pebble to his pocket. The forest video wallpaper was replaced with boring white walls. Instead of the face of the usual counsellor, he saw the round purple face of the architexter.

"Good cycle, Yar'oma," said Timofey Hesley. "How are you?"

"I am fine, sir. Thank you. What about you?"

"Frankly, I could be better if I did not have to attend this part of my duty, which is far from my favourite. But thank you for asking. Let's go through the formalities first and then have a chat. Okay?"

"Sure, Master Architexter." Yar'oma shrugged.

"In a few hours, you will go home. Tell me, Yar'oma Grinsky, how do you differ from the boy who walked into this room last Friday?"

"I don't. I'm the same person," answered Yar'oma. "Although, I lost a few cycles of productive study, and now I have to start two of my projects from scratch."

The architexter smiled. "Then what is the outcome of your rehabilitation?"

"I still would protect my brother if I had to. But if I have a chance, I will try to prevent the fight as much as possible."

"What if that makes you look like a coward or weakling?"

"Sir." Yar'oma leaned forwards a little. "I never cared how I looked ever since my father showed me what historically famous people of Earth used to look like, both on the outside and inside. Perhaps for this very reason, some of them did not end up in oblivion and are still remembered by O'Teka. Well, as long as I don't make people uncomfortable being near me."

"I see. The purpose of rehabilitation was to reflect and understand what you did wrong, why you did it, and why you should never do it. Do you understand that you might not be offered a second chance if you break the rules again?"

"I do."

"Do you know that you will no longer stay in the city and will be exiled into the Wildlands with minimal possessions and no colonial technology?"

"Yes, sir."

"You would have to learn to live either on your own or with the villagers, who are highly religious and live according to completely different laws."

"I am aware of that, sir."

"In that case, you are ready to go home after dinner. You gave me all the answers I expected from a boy your age, but I have another question for you."

"I am ready to reply, sir."

"Why permafrost?"

Yar'oma did not answer right away. He lowered his eyes and said, "Sir, to explain that even to myself, I must learn the truth about my origin. I need to know if I really was born of svoloch. My father keeps saying that I am too young to learn the story of my birth, but Dmitro once said something he didn't mean to. It stuck with me."

"Why don't you just wait?"

"Because it's painful. **Especially since the permafrost called.**"

"It would be wrong to break my rules as an architexter and tell you your story. But I can assure you that both of your parents had no more svoloch genes than most of us, including me. Physically, your mother was human, a third or fourth generation of second-wave earthlings."

"And my biological father? I know I am adopted."

"Your father was a true Novercian. You inherited his colours and his build. The rest about how you came to be will be learned in good time."

"Then my attraction to permafrost was simply manifested by imagination. And no, I don't want to go there any longer."

"Good," Timofey said joyfully, "I'll see you outside when you come to the temple for your school. Say hello to Obydva for me."

The screen went blank, but the boy jumped up, exclaiming, "Wait! What do you mean 'physically'? Who was my mother . . ."

But once again, Yar'oma was alone in the black forest, and tiny white flakes slowly fell through the rays of reddish light.

***

Obydva knew his son would ask him this question sooner or later.

"Dad, have you noticed how Yar has changed?"

"He was always quiet, Dmitro," Obydva said without looking up from the chopping board.

"No, he is worse than usual. We hardly see him. I wake up early, and he's already gone out. He stopped using the gym, doesn't pop in for lunch, and returns when we're already asleep. Especially since our rehabilitation, you stopped singing songs with us and praying stories out loud. We still need to finish *The Mysterious Island*. Only on weekends is he here, and then he sits in his room or the garden with his borrowed bibles and hardly talks. Where does he spend all his time?"

"In O'Teka's temple, of course, and sometimes in the workshop of Master Doro."

"Is there something wrong with him?" Dmitro asked. "He's no longer just an introvert but a real city hermit. He will soon be sleeping in the archives. How can we help him?"

"And what makes you think he needs help? Yar is your brother; he loves you and is loyal to you. He has proven it more than once. Let him be."

Dmitro's face frowned even more. He said, "Are you sure he's not going crazy? Maybe it's my turn to take care of him now?"

Obydva wiped his hands on the kitchen towel and patted the boy on the shoulder. "I'll talk to him myself first. Where is he now?"

"He's sitting in the garden in our wickiup."

Obydva told his son to wait for him in the house and went out through the side door. In the far corner of the garden, overgrown with wine currant and tundberry bushes, stood a low structure made of branches and dry grass, which the boys had built when they were eight.

Yar'oma sat inside on a cushion taken from a garden chair with his school terminal, the size of a dinner plate, and stared at the holo-screen with his silver eyes, not even blinking when Obydva crawled on all fours into the hut and sat down next to him.

"Praying?"

"No," Yar'oma replied. "I downloaded the wrong bible and am now looking for additional material in the school catalogue."

"Which material, if it's not a secret?"

"Anything about the *Lyra-4* mission."

"It won't be in the school catalogue. Maybe only the first mentions of the 'Object' in the Platinum Age Earth Encyclopaedia."

"I've already prayed those volumes." Yar'oma raised his head and looked at his father. "Can you find something for me with your amulet?"

"I'm afraid not. Nathaniel Alloyway's works will be available to you in a few years. Still, the bible you're looking for is not stored in O'Teka's archives. It exists only in the personal library of the first architexter. That is, in their head."

"You mean Architexter Vist? But why? Doesn't O'Teka possess all knowledge?"

"No. That which was to be forgotten due to the author's punishment must either be destroyed or hidden in special circumstances. This burden lies on the shoulders of the first architexter and no one else."

"I see. And if Vist dies, will this knowledge be lost forever?"

"If his alternate can upload it to their neuropath, then it will be their decision and responsibility."

"So this is the only way to access it? No one can see it until the first architexter is dead?"

"Yes. Why are you asking such strange questions?"

Yar'oma shrugged. "I'm not sure. It must be my whim tempting me with mysteries. Father, tell me about the first architexter. Who is

Vist? I have only seen him once in the temple. He does not look like an ancient elder. Is it true you have known him for many generations? Him . . . or her. Am I right?"

Obydva sighed, touching his shaved head with his large palm. "Vist is . . . many things. And many people, not just one. It is about how that beautiful body was created and how that great mind was built. It is similar to how I came to be, but much more complex and ancient. You also have something in common with Vist. A sibling to care for. The only way Vist's brother or sister now exists is in Vist's head. I don't know if Vist is a man or a woman, but I have a reason to suspect that Vist has the freedom to be anything he or she wants every few years. I could be wrong, but being a loader myself makes me think anything is possible with Vist. The first architexter has always been good for people, but only when people want to improve. Vist has a way of looking after themself, so everyone else is better off. Vist gave us all a chance to survive as human races should, for everyone to find a purpose and live a happy, fulfilled life. One cycle, you will have a purpose and understand how important it is to live by reason and effort. Do you know what you would like to be in the future?"

"Father, I want to be a loader."

5 Part 5. *Wasp* the Spaceship

The old spaceship didn't take long to arrive at the unknown continent.

Further from the water, the dunes were higher and drier. The wind wasn't as strong as Nat expected, and the coral-coloured sand was fine and light, like ground paprika. It creaked underfoot and sparkled slightly with grains of mica and quartz.

They landed on this deserted beach because they found Tom Darkwood's shoe. The scanners detected a chain of fairly large stones lined up in a long row. They almost missed it because the wind kept scattering the reddish sand in all directions, miraculously failing to hide the almost perfectly straight line under the dunes. Either the boulders were high enough, or someone periodically swept the sand away, but they explicitly resembled a signal. Therefore, Nat decided to land the *Wasp* on a sharp cape that protruded far into the sea, looking like a long tongue. A strip of stones cut it off from the rest of the shore.

They exited the ship and came closer to the stones to investigate. It was then that they saw a stick stuck in the middle of the stone strip with a scout boot made of ucha-silk on it. Nat recognised it immediately, grabbed the boot and started to examine it.

At first, he yelped and dropped the shoe because a creature, similar to an insect but without segmented legs, crawled out of it and disappeared into the sand. Then Nat put his hand into the shoe and pulled out the insole. Written on the insole were the words: "Technology beyond this line is strictly prohibited. Tom."

This message was too inappropriate as a joke and too incomprehensible to ignore. However, it was the second and more convincing sign that Tom had survived the incident. It did not prove he was still alive, so they left the celebration for later. Landing on the peninsula was a good choice, as it obeyed the warning in the shoe.

Nat left the boot for Irida to analyse, and he, accompanied by Hans, crossed the chamber border.

After climbing the hill, Nat looked around. He saw nothing except a group of dark rocks and an endless desert.

"Sir, are you okay?" Hans asked.

"Why do you ask?" Nat replied.

"You're breathing oddly and moving as if there's a weight tied to your legs."

Nat intended to protest, but after listening to his body, he was forced to admit that his first officer was correct. For the first time, Nat became aware of the heat in the air and his overwhelming fatigue. This was perplexing, considering his few implants that should have maintained his loader's homeostasis.

"I am fine; I'll manage. Let's investigate those rocks over there. I see no footprints; the wind obliterates them with sand. But if there were any, they'd lead to the nearest shadow." Nat cleared his throat, spat out the sand in his mouth, and added, "And the nearest shadow is right there."

He took two steps towards the rocks, fell and lost consciousness.

***

Nat opened his eyes; stars flashed through the air around him. He could not get up, could not even move. Smoke filled his lungs. He coughed and spat; his ears were still ringing from the explosion. That bomb destroyed the crater, the old spaceship, but the stench of the svolochs' dwelling was still in the air. The svoloch could not survive such a blast. Maybe another loader could, and – of course – it didn't work.

Nat raised his head and listened. These were human steps approaching him confidently but slowly. Nothing could be seen in the mixture of smoke and fog. Nat rose to his full height, cursing the pain in his back, and prepared to fire. In the white cloud, a shapeless silhouette first appeared, which took on the outline of a human of short stature and wide clothing with a hood thrown back. The approaching person looked beneath their feet and tried not to step on the corpses.

At the sight of the figure in a robe with thick locks of chestnut hair, Nat cried joyfully, wanting to grab the loader in his arms. But he restrained himself and only asked with a tremor in his voice, "Vist?"

The olive eyes turned to him, and Nat realised he was mistaken. The resemblance was startling, but this face was younger, darker, with fuller lips and no shaved temple.

"No," a velvety feminine voice answered him. "I am the daughter of the person you are looking for."

"Daughter?" Nat mumbled in shock.

"Yes. Vist was my—"

The electric shock restarted Nat's heart and woke him up.

No! he wanted to scream before regaining full consciousness, then shouted "Take me back there; I need to ask where Vist is?"

But darkness enveloped him once again, this time without dreams.

***

He awoke in a bed in the *Wasp*'s medical room, surrounded by all four team members.

"Finally!" said Nelia.

"He's alive," said Hans with a grunt.

"And healthy?" asked Naoki, a smile on his face.

"Not quite," replied Irida, securing a drug administrator on Nat's upper arm. "The supporting inserts are functioning well, but there are instability issues. Their contact with internal organs is compromised. It's fortunate, Captain, that you pilot the *Wasp* manually."

Nat struggled to speak immediately but soon began to mumble, "*Wasp* is a relic, nearly as old as I am; we're both from Earth and relinquishing control would be a moral crime. What's wrong with me?"

"You've had a stroke. This is the first case in the last two hundred and sixty years. The loader's set of implants was meant to protect you, but you haven't had a heart transplant in eighty years. Cloned organs also wear out," said Irida.

"But am I okay?"

"So far, yes. I found a compatible spare in my frozen vitals bank. We were all worried sick about you, but the surgery was successful. You have a new heart, Captain Alloyway, but I lack the skills to connect it to the implants. You'll recover in about twenty hours and resume leadership, but your loadership is suspended until we take you to Darkwood Hospital."

"We need to start searching. Tom has to be nearby. When can I at least get up?"

"When I'm satisfied with your condition. Until then, Hans is in charge."

Knowing there was no use arguing with the ship's medic, Nat turned away from her with a frown.

"Hans, about those rocks . . ."

"Captain, after I brought you back to the ship, Nelia and I returned to the rocks. Our traces have already been erased. We found nothing around them. The scanners there don't work well, but I suspect there's something hidden in those stones. We have a new problem."

"What is it?"

"Our computer equipment works on board, but not beyond that stone boundary. Commander Darkwood's warning was justified. The areas behind it will have to be explored using primitive methods."

"We were lucky to find Tom's message. So we cannot move the *Wasp*?"

"No!" Nelia said with concern. "We almost lost you, Captain, and we might lose the *Wasp* if we move it to the area where technology does not work."

Nat thought for a moment. "So, we must do what we did on Earth before the Platinum Age."

"You're the only true earthling among us. If I'm not mistaken, you were also a scout," remarked Naoki.

"On Earth, I was a hunter. When Irida allows me, I'll come to you with a bunch of ideas about what can be done. It won't be what you're accustomed to."

"We'll await your suggestions."

"No need to wait. If Tom left any other of his gears nearby, the concentration of metals in them will be abnormal for this area. Nelia, you must first construct a simple metal detector. We may find another shoe or — "

Irida said, "That's enough. Hans's report has been uploaded to the O'Teka file, and you, my Captain, will view it tomorrow. Right now, you need rest."

She activated the medicinal patch on Nat's shoulder for regular doses and quickly dispersed everyone to their resting cabins. Despite his concerns, Nat soon fell asleep.

***

Half a metre below the surface, the red sand was damp and more compact than its loose top layer. Hans had dug a hole near a part of the rock seemingly broken off from the main stone and was leaning against it, on the verge of abandoning the seemingly futile task. Suddenly, his scout shovel struck the base of the rock, emitting a new metallic sound. Crouching down, he began clearing away the sand with his hands. Naoki also heard the ringing; he lay on his stomach to peer into the hole.

"This is a mechanism inserted right into the rock. I can't discern any purpose other than altering its position," Naoki observed.

"Why the fancy words? I say we've found the door," Hans commented.

"I prefer the scientific language used in O'Teka's reports, both mine and others."

"All right, how does this door open?" Hans prodded the mechanism with his foot.

"I don't know, but now there's a reason to test the rocks themselves for metal. The mechanism and door hinges might be beneath the sand, but will you dig up the door handle every time you need to use it? It should be accessible. Now, let's see . . ."

Hans looked up, but Naoki's head was no longer visible over the edge. Climbing out, he saw that his friend was already sweeping the metal detector along the stone wall.

The rock was a variegated mix of grey, white, black and red inclusions, golden veins and porous depressions. It resembled a slice of baked fruit cake, with various nuts and fruits mixed in the spongy dough.

"I didn't find the doorknob, but it looks like I found the keyhole," Naoki said cheerfully, overpowering the metal detector's squeal.

He switched off the crudely mounted instrument and set it on the sand.

Both scouts bent down, their heads nearly touching, to peer into a hole they hadn't noticed before amid the diversity and unevenness of the rock. It was round, about one and a half metres above the sandy surface, resembling other imprints of bubbles once filled with gas millions of years ago. However, this particular hole was deeper, with non-sharp edges. Its diameter measured ten centimetres, but its depth was obscured by the dense Novercian shadow and the rock's blackness. Despite their scrutiny, they couldn't discern any signs of metal.

Naoki, intending to explore further, was about to place his thin and graceful hand inside when Hans intervened, shining a flashlight into the hole.

"Careful," Hans warned, "Once, as a child, I stuck my hand into a clay hole and found a nest of goon-flies. I barely escaped and lost two cycles of my busy life on a hospital bed."

"Goon-flies don't inhabit these parts."

"How do you know what bugs live around here? The one we saw on the beach looked nusty enough."

Naoki shrugged. "I don't know, but if goons did, we would have already discovered gnawed skeletons. If not of the crew of *Skipper* the avion, then at least of Captain Tom, not far from his sign. Where there are goon-flies, there are always animal skeletons, cleaned to a white shine."

"Animals? Don't rush to conclusions, Mr Biologist. Perhaps we are yet to find them. But since I don't see any bugs, you can go in. My hand won't fit."

However, Naoki found nothing useful in the hole. "We don't have the key, and we don't have a rug under which it could be hidden either," he remarked. "What are we going to do?"

"Think," replied Hans, heading back to the camp tent. Both scouts sat on the mat, seeking refuge from the wind and scorching sun. They drank water, and after a few minutes, Hans resumed examining the rock and sand around them. Naoki decided to experiment. He inserted pebbles, metal items, and various objects into the hole. Finally, he poured water from a bottle, saying, "What if it should be filled with rain? Hey, Hans! Look! It's a funnel! It must be going into a narrow pipe. Would you fancy that?"

He did not really expect the result. Water permeated the porous rock. The exposed mechanism in the sand came to life with a creaking, and the rock rotated several degrees. A gap wide enough for a person to squeeze through emerged between it and the main cliff. As both scouts peered inside, they discovered stone stairs descending between the stone walls.

Naoki let out a whistle, "Handmade work! Hans, do you believe this was constructed before humans arrived here?"

"By whom?"

"Exactly."

"No. Captain Darkwood could have used a zapper to cut the stone into blocks and . . ." Hans paused.

"And personally excavated this sand, building the walls and stairs alone in an area where his implants don't work?" Naoki concluded. "Really?"

"He's an ancient loader. You've seen what they're capable of."

"Our captain is confined to a medical bed, struggling to control his ageing bones properly. His implants are malfunctioning. What if all the loaders are malfunctioning here? That could be why they haven't returned. Hans!" Naoki looked at his friend without a smile, a rare occurrence. "They couldn't."

"Now we understand why Nelia told us to take it easy. But that doesn't help us make sense of this structure."

"Should we descend?" Naoki asked.

"We should not. What's the matter with you? You never forget rules. We must inform the others, but the com-amulet isn't working from here. Let's head back. I'm hungry."

Shortly after their departure, the stone door above the unilluminated stairs came into motion and slowly sealed shut, the wind filling the pit and cracks with sand. Once again, the place appeared like no human foot had ever touched it.

***

Nat felt better as the four of them descended the mysterious stairs, escaping the harsh sun. He insisted on tagging along, ordering Naoki to handle the water in the "keyhole" and to keep the "door" open.

The stone steps were low and flat and looked so ancient and worn that there was no doubt that they had been built not by Vist or even by Tom but by someone else long ago.

The spherical lanterns in the hands of travellers illuminated the wet steps, which, after a couple of minutes of descending along them, led to the water. This place looked like an ancient but flooded dungeon.

"Just as I suspected. The water level here can't be below sea level," remarked Irida, tossing her torch into the water.

It slowly rolled down the steps further in. Unlike ocean water, this water without plankton was not green but clear as a baby's tear.

The bright spot of the sinking lantern stopped a few metres below the surface. Hans scooped some water with his hand and sighed: "At least the water here is cooler."

Irida removed her gears from her belt and prepared to dive. "Looks like I'll be useful here. If I don't return in twelve minutes, don't follow. Just wait. And if I do—"

"Then we all swim further," Nelia said.

Returning sooner than expected, Irida returned a torch and . . . a worn-out scout boot. When her lips were above the surface, she said, "The exit is about sixteen metres away, in a cave with a lake and a small island. Captain, does this boot also belong to Thomas Darkwood?"

Nat inspected the findings. "We have a pair. I have no doubt Tom also left it for us to find."

"Yes. It was strategically placed for the lantern to illuminate upon entry," Irida noted, concerned. "Are you up for the swim, Captain?"

"I'll manage," Nat replied, but Hans intervened, descending into the water first.

"Nelia and I will assist you, sir. Don't worry," Hans assured Nat.

The loader didn't object. He took a deep breath and was surprised at how small his lung capacity seemed. He agreed to relax and allowed his comrades to carry him under the water, like a river current. A few seconds later, they reached the other end of the tunnel.

The island Irida described earlier was small and uncomfortable to stand on. Sharp boulders were everywhere, and rectangular blocks were dumped on it and in the water, as if they were construction debris. Beyond, the lanterns revealed a lake of the same crystal-clear water, veiled lightly with warm vapour. The cave extended like a corridor into the darkness of the rocky folds.

"Hello!" Hans's booming voice echoed through the cave, and both women shushed him together.

"Now, why did you do that? You nearly deafened me," his wife grumbled.

"Hans, we have no idea how stable these rocks are," Irida cautioned.

But Nat thought he heard a nearby splash, likely a rock fragment dislodging and plunging into the water.

Yet, the splash repeated, drawing all the lanterns' beams in one direction. The water's clarity was astounding; even Nat could discern the round, whitish form and three beautiful, gemlike eyes. After a brief hesitation, the creature decided to emerge onto the island, its heavy waddling gait causing streams of water to cascade from its body back into the lake. Everyone took a cautious step back, observing the peculiar being.

"What in the world is this?" Hans asked.

"Hello there, little fella!" said Irida.

"He's even shorter than Noridans," remarked Nelia.

Nat now felt blind compared to his comrades, not due to the cave's darkness, but because his right eye had recently clouded over. Its synthetic neurons were failing, and the organic ones sent distorted signals, making it seem like he was peering through dirty glasses. Meanwhile, his left eye, equipped with a spherical camera instead of a natural eyeball, was dead.

His crewmates were considerably younger, relying only on temporary implants in their muscular systems and resorting to sensory amplifiers solely in extreme situations.

"Describe it to me," Nat said to Irida, closing his eyelids.

"This little guy looks like the blobster, with the same loose pale skin, three fish eyes and a similar beak under the folds of his chin. He is so round that his neck is gone, and his tentacles are more like the arms and legs of the dancers in the Carib Sumo Show, only this guy has three legs and three arms. What a beautiful, remarkable creature!"

"So, you're suggesting it's an upright blobster capable of walking on land?"

"I wouldn't call it a walk. He rather hobbles. It was easier for him in the water," Irida said. Then, turning to Nat, she asked, "Sir, did Captain Darkwood know our language? I mean, the language of the Ikhtees?"

Nat thought for a moment. "I highly doubt it. However, his son had friends from various races in college. Tom and Zina were quite social. Those students could have taught him a few words, depending on how often they visited their house."

"Well, then they definitely taught him to pronounce his name."

Nat reopened his eyes. The round creature stood before them, shifting from tentacle to tentacle. Irida lifted Tom's shoe again. The forelimbs, which might be called arms, rose to what might be called the chest, and the numerous extensions, which might be called fingers, curled into balls. Five small extensions on each hand began to form three letters repeatedly in the underwater language of the Ikhtees: Tom. Tom. Tom.

Irida, Nelia, and Hans each signed their names with their fingers, and the creature responded by showing two letters: *JJ*. It could have been its name or simply an acknowledgement. Nat initially struggled to recall the necessary letters, but then he raised his hands and, in the same underwater language, said "Nat."

The humanoid blobster widened its eyes even further, and its fingers fanned out and fluttered. It emitted a sound reminiscent of plucking a guitar string.

"Wow, Captain! It knows you," remarked Hans.

However, the creature, repeating Nat's name twice, turned around and plopped back into the water, disappearing instantly. As the dark water of the cave lake settled, Hans located a suitable stone beam and dragged it closer to the shore. Irida and Nelia assisted Nat in getting comfortable on its flat surface. They decided to wait, with the impression that the three-legged blobster hadn't simply fled without saying goodbye, and would return.

They waited for about forty minutes, talking and thinking of different theories. Hans speculated that Tom might have been consumed by walking blobsters or sacrificed to their rare specimen collectors. Irida argued that the blobster's behaviour suggested a civilised and rational being, although unfamiliar with human customs. Nelia concurred, noting that the creature had encountered people before, though the specifics remained unclear. Meanwhile, Nat had a nap and refrained from participating in the discussion.

They heard a distant splash as they contemplated their next steps if the creature failed to return. From the rocky tunnel at the opposite end of the lake emerged a light – not electric, but reminiscent of the glow emitted by oil or pink wax burners, similar to the ancient lanterns of Earth.

As Nat listened to the description of what his companions observed next, he lowered his head and spoke, his voice now feeble and strained. "There were legends on Earth about a ferryman, who, much like this figure, possessed an ugly boat and a lantern. Dressed in black rags, he would slowly row with an oar, ferrying departed souls into the fog, from whence they would never return, across the stagnant waters that separate the realms of the living from the realm of the dead."

A peculiar boat drifted ashore, guided by a human wielding the oar. The boat's material was indiscernible, while the man was clad in tattered fabric and remnants of ucha clothing. Over his head and shoulders hung what appeared to be a cloth woven from seaweed, abundant along the continent's shore.

"This man is not Tom," Nelia remarked, "He cannot be."

As the boat gently bumped against the rocks, the man rested the oar across his knees. His hands were large, with knobbly joints and black nails, some fingers bandaged in dirty rags. His left arm was visibly weaker and used with great care.

Nat rose from the stone beam and approached the water's edge. Raising the lantern, he peered into the weathered face, which studied him back with a single foggy eye nestled in a deep socket; the colour of the pupil was indiscernible. The second eye was covered by a thick, convex lens smeared with something to darken the light of Vitr, affixed to a leather strap. Thus, two almost one-eyed individuals locked gazes until three beautiful, healthy blobster eyes emerged from the water beside the boat.

Grinning, the man in the boat raised a hand and pulled the cloth from his forehead, revealing a bare skull with sparse grey hair threads.

"Tom?" Nat asked in disbelief. How could this frail, skeletal old man be the once vibrant, full-of-life Captain Darkwood? Surely, he couldn't have changed so drastically in just seventeen years. He should have experienced regular tissue regeneration like other heavily genetically altered earthlings. But Nat immediately remembered that lately, he had often been grabbing his lower back and experiencing other inconveniences when relieving himself. And this was just in a few cycles. Tom had lived here for nearly half a generation and now appeared to be an earthling a hundred and fifty years old.

"Look who's talking," came the voice, even weaker and creakier. "My eyes are as bad as they once used to be, but I can see, Nat, that you don't exactly resemble a fresh rosebud either. Hey, your white hair suits you better than ever."

Nat remained uncertain. "If you truly are Tom, tell me how we first met."

"You nearly shot me with your crossbow under the tower of St David's Cathedral. I see, you found my beacons," Tom said, nodding towards the shoe on the ground nearby. "What took you so long?"

"But how . . ." Nat started, bewildered, then stopped, his head shaking.

"I'll explain everything later. For now, we must leave this area. It's not safe for any of us here. You, my *old* friend, must join me in the boat, but everyone else must swim with JJ. Don't worry; he won't let you drown. And I'd like my shoes back, please. Thank you. Why did you have to get them wet?"

"Wait a moment, sir," Irida said, stepping forwards. "We have a young man outside at the entrance. He's keeping the door open for us."

"Then go fetch him, girl, if you want him to stay youthful. Don't fret about the door. I have another route to the surface," said Tom Darkwood, as it was him indeed.

***

Nat examined the strange structure with genuine amazement. If it hadn't been shown to him by his old friend Tom Darkwood but had, instead, been stumbled upon in these parts, he wouldn't have believed it was crafted by human hands. The material used to construct this raft or catamaran was the same as that used in Tom's small gondola, in which Nat now sat, holding on to the sides. The long, flat, whitish boards weren't made of wood – no trees grew in these parts – but cartilage. Most of all, they looked like shark bones. According to Tom, the vessel he was working on was built around a large skeleton of some unseen sea monster. It was lying in the same place where Tom had found it. Or rather, where it had been shown to him.

"What's this?" asked Hans, who swam to the right of the boat. His generation had seen large earthly fish and stingrays only in video illustrations on the encyclopaedia floors in the O'Teka temple.

"The blobsters call this creature with signs that in the Ikhtees' language would sound like Ra-Jillekroo. So, I called it Jill for convenience. Judging by some mineralised remains in caves, it's quite an ancient species and had changed little over hundreds of years, but I could be wrong for hundreds of reasons," Tom answered, mooring to the rocky shore.

"It's a big one," said Nat, "and you used its remains as a frame for a raft."

"This one is just a whitebait. An adult beast would not fit in this bay. One of them nearly drowned me the cycle you and I had breakfast together for the last time."

The journey here from the cave was short. On the way, Tom, who had not seen people for a long time, was glad to be introduced to four new friends. They emerged from the stone tunnel into the north-eastern bay, shielded from the scorching rays of Vitr and storms by a high cave arch that hung over them like a bird's wing. The area offered cool shade and wet red sand. Something else was there, but Nat couldn't figure out what.

Blobster JJ swiftly swam away after completing its task. Nat's crew exited the water, activating the dryers in their suits, and attempted to assist their captain out of the boat. However, Nat declined their support and followed Tom himself.

"Thank you, I'm feeling much better," he said.

As Tom walked towards the group of huge salt spheres, he chuckled without turning around, "Of course you do. This is the only place on the mainland where your implants function and tissue regeneration resumes. Unfortunately, it's too late for me; it merely keeps me alive."

Approaching a sphere the size of a house, he invited everyone to enter the opening cut out by a zapper. Inside the spacious round room was a floor, a table, a bed made of stone slabs, and other furniture crafted from the bones of sea animals, shells and dried ocean plants.

"Two crazy blobsters keep trying to decorate my house in their own style. Look what they did to my wall." Tom extended his finger to an intricate mosaic of translucent stones resembling greenish amber interspersed with plankton clusters.

"I think it's beautiful," said Nelia. "Look, Irida, it's blobster's art."

"Well, Mrs Korub, at least someone likes it. They stick them to the wall with their spit. I didn't try to dissuade them, although I would have preferred if they brought me oysters instead."

Tom instructed everyone to get comfortable, seated Nat at the table, and reclined himself on the bed covered with seaweed cushions.

"Sorry for my rudeness; I've grown weak," said Tom, "But I know the first thing I must do is tell you . . . and especially you, Nat, what happened to me that cycle when the ground literally disappeared from under my feet. It was Jill – not only is it fully grown, but also probably the oldest. Your comrades perhaps don't know, but you remember the sea serpent from Earth mythology. There it was in fairy tales, but here . . . Hm. Imagine a snake enlarged a million times, beheaded, gutted and unrolled flat like a flounder. Ribs pointing in opposite directions. It feeds from Vitr, like your wife's roses, and swims not horizontally, but vertically," Tom raised his good hand, turned his palm edge down, and demonstrated how it swam.

"Jill was resting on the surface when we inadvertently startled her awake. The force of her sudden movement dragged me under the water through the funnel," Tom said.

Nat wanted to say something, but Tom waved him to stop with the same hand. "There's no need, Nat. There was nothing you could have done. Out of sheer panic, Jill's only claw caught onto me, taking me hundreds of kilometres within seconds. Neither of us could ascertain our direction at the time. Thankfully, the ucha-silk prevented my left arm from being torn off, but it never fully healed."

As Tom sat upright, he shrugged off his worn shirt, revealing a series of scars spanning his chest and side, each about twelve centimetres apart.

"*Noah*'s dragon! The famous big bad fish!" Nat said, surprised.

"Yes, indeed," Tom replied. "Fortunately, Jill had no ill intent towards me. She caught me like a goon-fly, and upon returning to her safe place, she shook me off to anchor herself to the deep corals. The current would have carried me further, but there was a chain of islands nearby, where I managed to crawl ashore and camped to rest from such a speedy journey. Surprisingly, I still had almost all of my gear with me. Of my equipment, I lost only the microwave heater. The first aid kit and zapper were still on my belts. I struggled to stop the bleeding and probably wouldn't have made it if it weren't for the intervention of some locals who arrived soon enough for their harvest. Blobsters and Jill share a symbiotic bond. She filters vast quantities of plankton, and they, in turn, tend to her needs. They took me into their caves and tended to my wounds. How we came to understand each other is a tale unto itself. Most of them quickly grew weary of my presence, harbouring little affection for humans. Only JJ and his mate Bak remained by my side. They brought me molluscs and plankton mush to eat while I recuperated and showed me their dwellings in cave lakes beneath the islands and the northern mainland. Their houses are a riot of colour, painted with pigments from local polyps. When I expressed a desire to return from the caves to the surface, they guided me through their passages to this part of the continent, though more for their convenience than mine. At that point, I knew I was far from Gera and decided to settle in as best as possible, hoping for a rescue."

Naoki, who had been silent until now, finally spoke up. "This is how you made the colourful message we received?" he asked timidly.

"So you stumbled upon one of them. Ha! Well, I'm certainly grateful that you did," Tom said, chuckling. "Here, in this cavern, I discovered a few small salt buoys, and upon noticing my keen interest in them, the locals graciously provided me with enough big ones to make myself quite comfortable here, like the martyr in the salty village. Luckily, my zapper was still working. With it, I fashioned myself a home, a workshop and even a bathroom with a decent tub. They also gifted me their paints to decorate, which I used to send you my parts that started falling off. Losing teeth and hair bit by bit wasn't the first sign of ageing restarting, but it was supposed to be tangible proof of my continued existence. However, finding the right weather conditions for such signalling proved much more challenging."

"Your teeth?" Irida said excitedly. "So that's what was meant to be in your buoy. Unfortunately, it didn't arrive. The cavity in the painted sphere was empty."

"But you're here," Tom pointed out, "so at least one of them fulfilled its purpose."

"Commander, I'm eager to understand more about why you were undergoing these changes," Irida said. Captain Alloyway is the oldest among us. Are we to follow? Is it radiation or some disease? Do we need to leave this place as soon as possible, or can the cure be found here only? Can you shed some light on this anomaly and on why this spot seems safe for the implants?"

"In the early cycles, I began to notice the effects of the anomaly, though initially, I blamed my injuries," Tom said. "I'm afraid I don't have all the answers. The blobsters seem to have some understanding of it, but I never quite grasped their language well enough to comprehend their explanations fully. Young lady, you are an Ikhtees, aren't you? You may have better luck deciphering their messages before it affects us all. As a low-grade loader, the regenerative implants were my only advantage and are now my greatest loss. I've yearned to return home for some time now. My strength is gone, my arm is useless, and finding enough food has become increasingly risky. Unlike before, the blobsters don't visit me as frequently with supplies. I nearly lost the means to complete building my raft. JJ and Bak would only assist with its launch. Nat, I hope your boat is better than mine. Where is it?"

Nat listened to his friend's story with a heavy heart, feeling the weight of Tom's losses on these shores. He couldn't shake the sadness that gripped him, wondering if it was just empathy or if there was a genuine issue with his own heart mirroring Tom's decline. The once-stalwart captain now resembled a mere shadow of himself, his posture slumped and weariness evident in every movement.

In response to his question, Nat straightened up. "A boat?" he said, "We have a ship! Tom, you'll return home on the *Wasp*!"

For a moment, Tom nodded absent-mindedly, but then he stopped, pushing up his round goggles to peer at Nat with foggy eyes that seemed to see only a blur.

"My *Wasp*?" Tom said hoarsely. "So you . . ."

"Yes, I retrieved her from beneath the ice," Nat said. "Obydva devised a plan."

"This is more than I hoped for. I am sorry, but my mind is slow nowadays. I spent all this time talking about myself and did not ask the most important things. Is Obydva here? What about our guys? Is my Zina with you? And . . . Vist?"

***

Irida Pavlovic was less worried about her captain in this vast grotto. Nat looked a lot better. She knew this place somehow made his back stop hurting and even improved his eyesight. He rested with his old friend, Commander Darkwood, on a dry patch of sand in the shade. Naoki had already gone to the western shore to gather clams while Hans and Nelia awaited their next orders and watched Irida trying to talk to the blobsters. It was a challenging task, as Tom managed to teach them very little of her language.

The sea colonists of Noverca talked underwater using a language called the Silent Tongue. It evolved from Earth's ancient sign language. They called it that because a long time ago, before the Platinum Age, there were enough people with speech and hearing problems to develop almost their own unique culture based on their means of communication. However, all that had changed when everything considered an imperfection was removed from the human genome. Still, humanity safely preserved the language and all its teaching methods in the O'Teka temple archives. People thought keeping it along with many other dead languages was important, even though they were not used.

When artificial evolution produced the aquatic race of Ikhtees, some of the best linguists, led by the famous Mirr Varian in the White Capital, decided to resurrect the Silent

Tongue. They moulded the languages of the deaf and mute into one underwater language, adding bits from Noverca's vocabulary and some signs that didn't exist on Earth.

That's how the Ikhtees language was born. It was so beautiful and graceful – almost a dance – that to be fluent in it became a demonstration of respect among the other races in the Gera colony. But only the Ikhtees knew it well enough to create stories and songs.

Irida was born in an underwater city, Lantida. Both her parents were fourth-generation Ikhtees. Off the western shores of Gera, the seabed was a beautiful plain under the sea. People slowly grew a new part of the colony there, preferring the warm water to the hot land or frosty mountains. But Irida felt like she was born into the wrong race. Instead, she chose to be a dryland scout, which disappointed her clan a little.

Upon adulthood, several operations restored the girl's ability to live permanently in the air. Her combfin was also removed along the entire length from the bridge of the nose to the lower back. Still, she decided not to implant hair follicles and pheoletin pigment glands. She preferred to protect herself from the radiation of the cruel sun with a suit and a transparent helmet made especially for her by Master Andrea Alloyway. At the same time, she could immerse herself in water for a long time during visits to Lantida and she did not forget her native language.

Two blobsters and Irida twirled their fingers and tentacles in front of one another for a long time, and finally, she turned to her comrades, who were watching their conversation with interest.

"They not only have a scientific community but also their own temple with a collection of historical and artistic bibles in Vaaros. That is what they call their cave city," she said, "of course, I won't be able to read their works for a while since their language is quite complex."

"Hang on, miss," Tom said, "It sounds like they are using words I did not teach them. I don't know them myself in your language. I never heard of Vaaros."

Irida frowned in confusion, "I'm not sure what to say. They are not fluent, but the vocabulary is reasonable for simple explanations. I have no answer to this puzzle. Commanders, I'll have to go with them to at least look at the illustrations in their science labs. JJ says I'll understand more if I see their diagrams and layouts."

"Well, what can we do while we wait?" Hans said, turning to Nat with questions, "How are you feeling, sir?"

"I'm fine here, thank you. While in this grotto, the anomaly does not threaten us. Isn't that right, Irida?"

"I am sure that the regeneration-threatening problem concerns only Commander Darkwood and you, Captain. The four of us have not yet reached the age of needing to support ourselves with implants. All we seem to lose in these parts is our thermal vision, zooming iris and acute hearing. My friends also cannot sense moisture in the sand or accurately determine the direction during a storm. But we all have biologically inserted salt filters, and even without muscle implants, Hans and Nelia are very strong fighters."

Tom nodded. "That's it. In this case, I have a task for your young comrades, Nat. While your medical officer is swimming with the blobsters to that... Vaaros, we have things to do. Does your team know how to hunt?"

"They are scouts, the best King and McLeod Academy graduates. They can do anything," Nat answered.

Tom stood up and slowly walked towards the Korub couple, who then stepped towards him.

"Great!" Tom said, "Then this lovely pair will get us some meat since the anomaly doesn't threaten them. Young Naoki may have better eyes than me, but he won't find clams enough for all of us. It is better to make our way to the *Wasp* when we finish our business here to avoid going back and forth. It might be too bad for me. You two, go along the right shore from here. There is a path up to this hill. At the top, you will find a field with solarleafers. That's what I named the local flora. Under them, you can hide from the heat and find piggies. I call the very tasty creatures that live there 'pigs.' You won't confuse them with anything else when you see them. Don't touch the females; they are rare and a bit bony. Listen out for their mating song; they call every few hours. When you find the creature, wait. If males crawl to her, she will choose the fattest one, lay eggs under his skin and move on. Don't touch the impregnated one. He will hide in a hole, fertilise the eggs and feed himself to his young ones. Only one female will hatch from a dozen eggs, so if you see a male with a blue hump, let him be. Seek the rejected males. Believe me, one will be enough for us for a few cycles. The fastest way to kill it is with a zapper ray between its eyes ... There are actually no eyes there, but there are two dark spots on the neck. Although it's not a neck ... Well, you'll figure it out. In the meantime, Nat will tell me what I missed over the years," He turned to Irida again. "Miss Pavlovic, is your suit adequately equipped?"

Instead of answering, Irida touched both boots, and their soles began to extend forwards, turning into flippers. "I don't swim too fast without my combfin, but I hope to turn around soon, regardless of what I find out," Irida said.

After receiving some useful tips and a list of words Tom had learned in the blobster language, Irida disappeared with blobsters into the green wave.

***

Soon, Irida stretched her body to its limits and closed her eyes, finding it easier to tolerate the speed with which Bak dragged her through the thick green water. She felt the plankton exfoliating her face, and hoped she would have enough skin left to recognise herself in the mirror when all this was over. Fortunately, this sprint didn't last long, and soon Bak released Irida from the knot of tentacles. She opened her eyes and saw the water's surface directly above her head. Irida swam up and found herself at the entrance to a cave, similar to the corridor they had all sailed through behind Tom Darkwood's boat.

Bak indicated that she was welcome in the cave. There was no need to rush now, and she could look around and admire both the underwater and surface parts of the blobster's town, Vaaros. Although, that could be just their understanding of the real name.

There was plenty to admire. First, there was light here, which, to Irida's surprise, resembled the light produced by some deepwater organisms. Salt spheres rested on every rock ledge, their light softly shining from within. They ranged in size from large to small sea melons, arranged on both sides of the long, but reasonably broad, lake almost free of plankton. Bak slowly swam by her side, apparently understanding that Irida was marvelling at the sight. Soon, she saw the first structures decorated in bright colours. Osmanthus Carib's desserts came to Irida's mind. She couldn't figure out what the houses were made of. However, she suspected that the translucent material was most likely the organic product of living creatures, similar to terrestrial corals or sponges. However, the strength and shape were completely alien. Irida decided that this civilised species of blobsters had gone further and were building not salt spheres but houses from crystallised salts, sparkling in the soft light.

Diving down, Irida saw that the city continued underwater, and she concluded that the water level here was constantly changing due to the tides. The blobsters obviously preferred to conduct their business in the underwater part. They paid little attention to her or to Bak's unfamiliar signs. Apparently, her guide didn't want to waste any more time on the tour and led Irida to what could be a blobster's library. From a distance, it looked like a whole forest of thin and thick yellowish columns connecting the illuminated vaults of the cave and the lake bottom, just invisible to her in the darkness of the depth. When Irida found herself surrounded by these parallel columns, she did not understand at first why they were being so insistently shown to her. But she soon realised that they were not a natural creation but a craft of the inhabitants of Vaaros. These columns turned out to be blobster's books. Buk showed her how to read them by slowly moving around one of the columns in a spiral, ascending from bottom to top, as if the words were a ribbon wrapping a wide cylinder with a diameter of almost a metre. Irida noticed several other creatures in the distance who were showing similar behaviour. Readers?

Of course, Irida could not read what was written on those columns. Incomprehensible patterns, the inclusions of some fibres, sand grains, tiny air bubbles and pigment stains had been inserted into this yellowish crystal, like into decorative glass, forever frozen in it.

Bak waited patiently while Irida studied the vast translucent volumes and then urged her, with signs, to continue to follow him. She obediently swam after him, wondering what he wanted to show her this time. Finally, he led her to the edge of a cave lake, the shore of which moved steeply upward, almost to the very ceiling, with a similar staircase to the one Hans and Naoki had found in the sands, but in zigzags here. However, what surprised Irida most of all was the sign near the bottom step. The word "smucilage" was burned into the flat stone with a zapper.

Irida didn't know what should have shocked her more: the word written in human language (Tom Darkwood could have done this, and that was worth mentioning, in her opinion) or the realisation that all the things she had seen in the town, save for the stone slabs of the steps and platforms, were made not only of salt but also of smucilage – the compound secreted by blobsters to stop salt from dissolving into the water.

The high concentration of different salts on this planet was always one of the challenges for colonists. There was too much of it in the seawater and soil. Even most rivers and lakes were salty. Water distillers were constructed for the settlements, and colonists underwent genetic modifications to expel excess salt from their bodies, a mechanism similar to that observed in certain Earth birds.

For blobsters, salts were the main building material. They probably used it to slowly build their houses, mixing it with dyes and secretion, so the whole of Vaaros looked like it was made from colourful caramel for children to play in. However, the cylindrical "volumes" of their temple were mainly made of smucilage, giving it a look of impure and rough glass or frozen oil interspersed with debris.

Bak's friend JJ awaited them near the sign. He appeared somewhat bloated and peculiar, and Irida only recognised him because Bak addressed him by name. However, her question was answered when JJ staggered and disgorged a heap of flat, wet and slimy pebbles and translucent smucilage shards onto the well-lit area in front of the stairs. Overcoming her revulsion, Irida squatted to inspect them closely. She discovered that the pebbles bore human words, while the shards were adorned with lines of stains reminiscent of sea foam left on the sand by the surf. These transparent pieces were exactly the same as those used to lay out the patterns in the round one in Tom's house. Picking up one black pebble inscribed with the word "water," Irida observed as Bak raised his tentacles and vocalised the word in the Ikhtees language. JJ rummaged through his pile for a while before producing an almost transparent piece of salt with a squiggle trapped in it. Gesturing with his tentacles, JJ depicted the symbol, which Irida duly repeated. Both blobsters appeared pleased with such a fast learner, and Irida sighed; the lesson had begun.

***

Hans paused, chewing with his eyes closed. "Tastes like—"

"Chick-tash?" Nelia said, picking up her bowl and spoon and inhaling the aroma of the hot stew. While they hunted, Naoki made a quick trip to the *Wasp* and fetched utensils and a Vitr-stove – a portable device capable of cooking and cooling food in the field.

"No," Hans replied, opening his eyes. "Not chicken or pork. More like . . . darling, what is that vegetable your mom serves to vegetarian guests?"

"Uzhanian jackfruit?" Nelia said.

"Exactly. Less chewy, more filling. I might replace my breakfast bacon with it, but not my Sunday roast," Hans replied.

Nelia took a spoonful. "You're just hungry. Bet you won't swap your crispy bacon for this." She tasted it. "Mmm, it's nice, but . . . reminds me of some fish."

"I disagree," said Naoki, "Fish would have been a real treat, but this meat is not bad either. It is rich in fat and protein, phosphorous – yes. Calcium – not so much, but the texture's like porcini mushrooms. Captain, what do you think?"

"How can you eat this at all? This is what I think. It's terrible," Nat said, setting down his bowl.

"At first, I felt the same." Tom Darkwood chuckled. "But Mrs Korub is right. Hunger can be quite persuasive. So, Nat, tell me about my granddaughter. Why did Boris name her Glaudia?"

But before Nat could respond, the blobsters JJ and Bak arrived and created almost a mini-storm in the small bay, and a young woman emerged from the foamy waves like Poseidon, holding a long staff instead of a trident.

"Guys, Ir is here!" Nelia said.

Naoki stood up. "We have a bowl of stew for you to try, Irida. It's made from that thing," he pointed at the mass of the shapeless carcass Hans had somehow managed to bring back to camp and butchered in the deep and cool shade of the grotto.

But Irida barely greeted them and hurried inside Tom's sphere. Intrigued, everyone followed after her. JJ and Bak didn't.

Irida stood by the wall decorated with the blobsters' "artwork." When Tom caught up with everyone else, she turned to him.

"Commander Darkwood, can you tell me when JJ and Bak made this mosaic? It wasn't too long ago, was it?"

"No, if I remember correctly, it was here for a few weeks," Tom replied, "That was when their behaviour changed; they became very enthusiastic for about a week. Soon after this 'redecoration,' they lost interest in me."

"And when did you last go to the lake city with them? To their library?" Irida asked.

"I haven't been ever since I left years ago, girl, and they never showed me their library," Tom explained. "I was their captive, and it was too early for me to study them. I needed to recover and survive first. Besides, Vaaros is several kilometres from this safe place, and I am too weak to travel the way they insist. All I wanted was to finish building my bone-raft and . . . to try to get to Gera."

"I understand. Still, you managed to learn a few words to communicate, which is better than nothing."

"I had very few words in common with them. More about food. I taught them to show my name and the names of those I expected to see again. Then, they brought a handful of pebbles and these pieces of their glass. I still didn't understand what they wanted from me, but they laid them out on the sand for a long time and repeated the words 'one' and 'two' many times. I thought that they were testing whether I could count, and I apparently completely confused them with my attempts to confirm that."

Commander, this is their writing," Irida pointed at the mosaic again. "Some of these stones carry human words, but your eyesight has failed you, and we did not look closely. They left this message for you. It said ... the closest to human will be '*One alone and one alone. Pain and death. Two are pleasure, future, life. Make a sign, find the sign. Be two.*' They tried to tell you that they found ... what they thought was your lost mate. They took pity on you because you are alone. Blobsters cannot exist alone. If one of the pair dies, the other suffers greatly. They thought you were building your big boat to find your mate. They see it as equivalent to their spheres. A few months ago, they found and brought another human to the Vaaros."

"Another human? But who? Vist?" Nat asked.

"I thought of the architexter, too!" Naoki added.

"Wait, Ir, have you learned to read in these few hours?" Hans asked, surprised.

"No, I found this!" Irida said, lifting and standing the staff upright. "They were really unhappy that I took it, but I promised to return it. This is a letter from Groonya. I also found her notes on various stones."

"What?" everyone exclaimed in disbelief.

"Is Groonya here?" Nat asked. "Where are the others? She was with Rod, Steven and Zina!"

When the flow of questions stopped, Irida told how, at first, she thought that the words on the pebbles and boulders were left by Tom, who, for some reason, forgot to tell her about them. But then she found this long fish bone. Upon closer inspection, everyone saw that it was covered from left to right and almost to the full length with words written in a spiral in colourful inks, which the blobster's city had in abundance.

Irida told her friends about the cylindrical books in the Vaaros temple and the inscriptions Groonya left on stones and small pebbles. But Irida didn't find Groonya herself in the cave. A small boat is hidden there, but Groonya is no longer in Vaaros. The blobsters explained that the "clever human" went off with another lonely human, who had come after her on the largest sphere that could fly.

Irida handed the bone to Naoki. "Please read this to all of us. Your eyes see better in such bright light."

The young man took the staff, found the beginning at the tip, and began to read, slowly turning the staff in his hands: "Cycle 42. Uncle Tom, greetings! I guess it's you that these guys keep telling me about every cycle. At least they repeat your name in Ikhtees more often than other words I assume you taught them. Although I have a small boat, I've been stuck in a cave for a week. Jellykids look after me, feed me with shellfish and plankton mousse, and tell me that you like them very much. When I try to return to the avion, where my father and the McLeods are waiting for me, they persistently repeat the word "danger" and do not let me out of this colourful cave, although they brought me here themselves. Cycle 66. This couple of Jellykids teaches me their language, just as parents teach a child. After two cycles of communicating with them, I began to write human words on small pebbles, and they rejoiced as if they did not know that people could also write. They immediately showed me their writing, and we finally started making progress. Cycle 82. I have learned that you are not far away and suffer loneliness. Also, I think I know why the loaders become so unwell here. This might have been an artificially created phenomenon, but I need to show my notes to Dr Zina, or even better, to the architexter, to be sure. Jellykids say that this is the legacy of their ancestors, who wanted these people to remain – the closest meanings of the words I picked up are "clean" and "even." (Sorry, I'm not fluent in the Silent Tongue.) This extensive field probably covers most, if not all, of the mainland and a group of nearby islands. The field is not continuous; there are pockets in it, and I believe that if you are still alive, you are staying in one of them."

Naoki read, turning the staff while everyone listened intently.

"Cycle 154. With great difficulty, I managed to explain to them that I wanted to see the source of this field. But they only showed me the direction further to the south and down. Probably underwater. A team of young Ikhtees scouts should have come here; they would have sorted it out. Tomorrow, I will try to persuade them to take me back to the island where Jellykid found and kidnapped me. I am desperate to regroup with my team.

"Cycle 167. Jellykid took me out of the cave on my boat with many precautions. I learned the word 'Monster.' We didn't get far before they got worried again, but I left a noticeable sign for the others to find me on one of the rocks."

Irida interrupted the reading. "I didn't spot it on the way in but found it before I came back here. She drew a huge purple and yellow letter G on the northern side of the cliff, close to the cave. I guess the avion landed on it, and the frightened blobsters gave her up easily. Please, Naoki, keep going."

"There isn't much left," said Naoki and continued reading. "Cycle 202. They won't take you this monstrous bone. They think everything written in the cave should stay in the cave, like in the temple. They also said no when I asked about other humans who might have come here. So, Vist and Mik haven't been to these parts. Their fate is still unknown. Only two Jellykids spend time with me. The rest don't show any interest."

Naoki stopped reading.

"Well?" Hans asked.

"That's it. The writing stops as if interrupted," said Naoki.

"So they must be alive and not far away and sitting still for the same reason we are," Nat said. "How did we miss them on the way here?"

"They also came from the north, but probably further east, following the chain of islands. Our course was a straight line," Hans said.

Nat replied, "We need to go back to the *Wasp* and look for them."

"No, Captain. *We* need to go and look for them," Nelia said, "You and Commander Tom should stay here until it is safe for us all to head home."

"I also found this thing. It was at the bottom of the lake." Irida pulled something from her wet pocket that looked like a piece of plastic, with a clear number 01 still visible on it.

"Could Groonya have dropped it? It looks human, but I don't recognise it."

"I do," said Tom. "This is a shard of the smashed cargo container that belonged either to *Noah-1* or *Arc-1*."

***

The boat Steven built for slender Groonya was too small for two large and muscular people like Nelia and Hans. Yet after JJ and Bak dragged them to the lake city of Vaaros, neither the blobsters nor the scouts wanted to repeat the experience. Nelia was glad that Hans had claimed the boat left by Groonya and decided to navigate it to the coordinates the girl had written in her notes. Only Naoki agreed to "ride" a blobster again towards the islands and the avion's location. Being lighter and more streamlined, it was less uncomfortable for him and JJ as long as he wore goggles and covered his head with ucha-silk for protection. Nelia and

Hans decided to try the boat.

"It's not as far as I thought. JJ took no more than ten minutes to bring me here from the commander's camp," Naoki said, standing waist-deep in the water just outside the cave. "I'd say I was dragged at a speed of about eighteen kilometres per hour, so we're no more than three kilometres from them now."

"Our implants do not measure speed and distance as accurately as they should, remember?" Nelia said, making something like a hood for Naoki with his ucha-silk shirt.

"Of course, but I was relying more on my perception."

"I don't know how you managed to stay conscious, never mind perceiving time and distance," Hans said, pushing the boat further away from the cave mouth.

Nelia covered Naoki's head and asked, "Are you comfortable?"

"Absolutely. The distance to *Skippers* that Groonya describes in her journal is almost three times as long. Thanks to you, ma'am, I'm sure I'll survive and will be there first."

"And we'll be right behind you." Hans got into the boat and tested the ZPE-engine. It didn't work.

"Looks like you won't—" Naoki started, but a well-rested JJ took off without warning, and the young man disappeared into the waves with a splash.

"Look at him go," Nelia said. "I hope he doesn't forget to pop up for air from time to time while he's measuring his speed."

"He'll be fine," Hans said, trying the engine again. "Well, my dear. Are you ready to go, or do you need more time in Vaaros with Irida? This boat needs some work done."

"Nah, we've already gone over the plan more than once. Let's go. We haven't been alone for a while. Here, I feel under constant three-eyed scrutiny. Let me have a go at that engine. I'm determined to fix it."

But after several attempts, it became clear that there was a severe malfunction in the zero-point energy device that couldn't be fixed without Nelia's tools left on the *Wasp*.

Bak slowly swam to the boat as the couple sat in it, sighing and looking at each other. Without saying a word, he began to push them into the sea. Beyond the surf, he wrapped his elongating tentacles around the boat's bow and towed it away from Vaaros.

"Is he really going to pull us all the way to *Skippers*?" Nelia asked.

"I hope so," her husband replied. "We have neither oars nor a motor. But if he leaves us in the middle of the ocean, we'll be carried south by the current, and we'll be boiled alive. Especially if we decide to swim. I don't know anything about the currents in these parts."

"Why do you think he would leave us?"

Hans sighed. "Because right now, I'm afraid of that more than anything."

Nelia smiled at him. "Don't be afraid, honey. These creatures do not wish us harm. Look how carefully and slowly he moves. He understands that the sides are not high."

"We're just too heavy for him alone, although the two of us wouldn't have been able to row faster. He'll get tired or bored, and then . . ."

At that moment, the boat rushed forwards, and Hans, sitting closer to the stern, yelped and fell overboard.

"Hans!" Nelia screamed as she saw her husband's head flash, a dark spot in the foam furrow. The vessel rushed off quickly like a speedboat. There was no point in yelling at the blobster to stop. Nelia crawled to the boat's bow and lay down on her stomach. She reached out with her hand to the tentacle, tightly gripping the boat's hull, and began tugging and punching it, trying to get Bak's attention. But it didn't help. She pulled out her scout blade and slashed the tentacle along the fibres. Nelia did not have time to think or feel sorry for the blobster, but it hadn't yet occurred to her to cut off a limb. The tentacle released the boat, which for some time still moved forwards. Nelia looked around but saw nothing except the sea.

She rushed to the stern, shouting her husband's name, but she didn't see anything in that direction either. In desperation, she raised her eyes to Vitr and tried to determine whether the boat was drifting in that direction or not, but due to her anxiety, she couldn't tell.

Nelia froze, half-squatting and clutching the boat's sides with both hands. In this uncomfortable position, she desperately waited for the unpleasant humming in her ears to go away, her heart to stop racing, and her breathing to even out. She wanted to close her eyes, but she was afraid of losing the last bit of control over her connection with the world, which in an instant had turned into a terrible and hungry emptiness, suffocatingly hot and hopeless.

The waves rocked the boat and knocked it on its sides, and alongside this noise, Nelia thought she heard a new sound. It was like a distant and short cough.

Nelia let go of the edges and stood up to her full height, peering intently in the direction from which she heard it. In the distance, either one of the waves got too playful, or something surfaced and dived again.

Looking around in the boat, Nelia saw that their flasks of water were still stuffed under the only bench, a plastic board twenty centimetres wide that served as a seat at the helm. Without hesitation, Nelia grabbed this board with both large hands and, growling like an animal, tore it out along with the screws that secured it in place. Using the board like an oar, she began to row in the direction that interested her more than anything else. It was not easy, but she was encouraged by the thought that she, although slowly, was moving north, away from hellish Vitr.

Soon, Nelia stopped and listened again. Then she put on her goggles, took a deep breath and plunged her face into the water, leaning over the side. The water temperature here must have been about thirty degrees. Despite the plankton swirling beneath the surface like green clouds, Nelia could make out a pale round mass just a few metres below her.

Puzzled, Nelia stood up and began rummaging through her travel bag. She quickly found what she was looking for – a coil of strong, thin cable. Nelia tied one end of the cable to the boat and fastened the other to the belt around her waist. As she took a few deep breaths, she said aloud, "Where is Irida when you need her?" and dived into the green ocean.

The lower she went, the less dense the plankton became and the clearer the water. Visibility didn't improve because it was darker down there. But the water was cooler, and Nelia saw a strange bell-shaped dome resembling a giant mushroom with grey matte sides and a very long and thin stem. She saw several other similar domes, but they were lower and several metres from each other.

"Underwater balloon – some kind of vegetation," Nelia decided, and was about to emerge when several air bubbles quickly rushed past her from the dome's edge to the surface, where they probably made that cough-like noise.

Knowing she couldn't hold her breath much longer, Nelia still decided to look under the dome, and the cable length was just enough to reach the edge. She saw darkness under the dome and turned on her shoulder torch. A bright beam illuminated the figure of a man lying motionless on the water, face up. The dome appeared to hold enough air to keep it from sinking, and it dangled on a thin stalk just below the clouds of plankton.

Nelia could not reach the surface of the air reserve under the dome since the length of the cable was just a little too short. But it was important and urgent to check whether Hans was alive. She couldn't reach him and decided to take risky action. A desperate woman unfastened the rope and let the boat drift. She dived under the dome with one wave of her strong arms, and a moment later, she saw her husband's face. He was alive but unconscious. He had not drowned. He breathed the air under the dome, and, despite the shallow breaths, he would soon run out of oxygen here.

Fear for his life gave her strength. Nelia grasped Hans under his arms and began pulling him from under the dome towards the sea surface. It was an arduous task; the resistance of the water and the weight of her unconscious husband slowed her down. But she pressed on, her determination fuelled by dread.

Breaking through the surface, she gasped for air. She quickly checked Hans's pulse and felt a weak but steady beat. Relieved, she positioned him so his head was above water and started swimming back to the boat. Her ribcage burned with the effort, but she pushed through the pain.

As she reached the boat, she climbed over the low boat side and, with a final surge of energy, managed to pull Hans in. She didn't know that she had barely managed to avoid a thousand fine threads reaching out to her to sting and drag them both back under the dome. Exhausted, she collapsed beside Hans, her chest heaving. She checked his breathing again, ensuring he was stable. Then, she lay there, staring at the sky, feeling the boat gently rocking beneath them.

After a few moments, Nelia sat up, gathered her remaining strength and examined her husband again. She could not understand why Hans was still unconscious if he was breathing and showed no signs of water in his lungs. Despite all her efforts and scout skills, he would not wake up. When she lifted his eyelids, she gasped in horror. Instead of his white eyes, she saw eyeballs filled with an opaque yellowish substance. Nelia felt sick for the first time in her life. She could not explain what she saw and did not know what to do. She noticed Hans's dark purple skin had become even darker, almost black, like their field uniforms.

The first thing that came to mind was that he might have been bitten by some poisonous sea creature. The plankton might have contained harmful microorganisms that entered his body. What if he swallowed plankton along with seawater? Then she remembered the domes. He had breathed the air under the dome for quite a long time. Nelia herself stayed there for less than a minute. How did Hans end up under the dome in the first place? Where does that air come from?

Nelia closed her eyes and tried to gather her thoughts. Let's say those mushrooms filter air from seawater. This would explain the presence of oxygen because plankton photosynthesise. But what if poisonous gases were in the water or the mushrooms produced toxins? What do these mushrooms feed on? Plankton, like many sea dwellers? Or sea dwellers themselves?

In any case, Hans needed help, and whether Nelia herself was in trouble was unknown. She turned her attention to the boat, preparing to row again for as long as she was alive. "Hang in there, Hans," she whispered, brushing a lock of wet hair from his forehead. "We'll get through this. Together."

Nelia had no idea where she was going from there. All she knew was that she had to move north, away from Vitr. She picked up the makeshift oar she had fashioned from the bench and began rowing, straining with each stroke to distance them from the toxic environment they had just escaped.

As she rowed, she kept an eye on the horizon, hoping to spot any sign of land or rescue. Her mind raced with questions about what had happened to Hans and how to save him. The boat's progress was painfully slow, but the rhythmic splashing of the oar broke the silence of the vast, empty sea.

How much time passed, she could not tell, and Vitr baked Nelia's back like an oven. Exhausted but determined, she continued to row, driven by the hope that they would find those islands, the avion *Skippers* and Doctor Zina within it. Nelia's muscles ached, and her hands were blistered, but she refused to stop. Every few minutes, she checked on Hans, hoping for any improvement. Occasionally, she sipped water from the flask and tried to pour a few drops into Hans's mouth, but he would not swallow.

"Hold on, Hans," she whispered from time to time. "We're almost there."

Three bottomless blobster eyes emerged from the water in front of the boat and slightly to the right side. Nelia stopped rowing.

"Bak?" she asked, forgetting this was not a way to speak to this species. The blobster raised its tentacles above the water, forming the word "monster" in the Silent Tongue. One of the tentacles was injured but not bleeding any more. It was Bak.

"Yes, I suppose I am," Nelia said aloud again. "I am sorry for cutting you, but I bet you would have done the same in my place."

Next to Bak, another round head with three eyes appeared closer to the boat. It looked like Naoki had already been delivered to their destination.

"Monster – under . . ." said JJ, adding a few more words Nelia did not understand.

But she surely knew one word in the Silent Tongue. "Help," Nelia said with her fingers.

Both blobsters disappeared into the waves.

"Fine!" Nelia breathed and picked up her oar. "You can eff off, too."

But the boat shook and started to move rapidly, slightly changing course towards the north-west. White tentacles wrapped it on both sides. Nelia clung to Hans, feeling the boat surge forwards with a new-found speed. The wind whipped through her hair, and she took a moment to enjoy the breeze despite the dire circumstances. She just hoped that the blobsters weren't taking her to her punishment.

Part 6 Time to Regroup

"I see my *Cutter*!" Steven said, pointing to a dark dot among the green sea waves. It rapidly grew larger, revealing Groonya's boat, which appeared to be empty.

The blobsters pulled the boat swiftly, but everyone on the island struggled to see it clearly without eye enhancement. Only Steven held something resembling a spyglass, which he had made when he and Zina searched for Groonya.

As *Cutter* approached the shore, the blobsters slowed and gently guided the boat to a small cove sheltered by rocky outcrops. With a final push, they brought the boat to rest on the sandy beach and returned to the sea, floating nearby on the surface as if waiting to see what would happen next.

Four people ran towards the boat. Naoki, whom Zina had just examined on the shore, was the first to reach *Cutter*. (A few hours after meeting Naoki on the island's beach, Zina noted that Groonya still did not trust him and hadn't let him near the *Skippers* avion). Limping and cursing at his body, Steven was the last to arrive. He saw a thin white tentacle from one of the blobsters rise out of the water and push Naoki away from the boat so roughly that, from a distance, it looked like a blow from a whip. Naoki stopped in surprise, bent down and examined something in the boat. When

Groonya caught up with him, he stopped her by raising his hand.

Zina and Steven also reached *Cutter* and saw two motionless bodies. A large woman seemed to be covering the body of a muscular man to protect it; both were unmoving.

"These are my friends Nelia and Hans Korubs," Naoki said in a shaking voice. "Master McLeod, you remember them from the scout academy."

"Hey," Steven shouted to the blobsters, "What did you do to them?"

Zina accompanied his words with hand gestures, from which Steven understood only "what" and "wrong." One blobster stuck its head out of the water and waved its limbs. Groonya translated the words "monster," "under" and "food" aloud, then watched it silently for a while, moving her lips. Finally, she turned to Zina. "In the annals of the lake city, I saw images of some living creatures carved into the columns, and I named them in the Silent Tongue for myself. I called one of them 'Parachutes' because of their similar shape. This Jellykid . . . I mean, this blobster repeats it now in his language in combination with other words. He seems to be saying that what I call a Parachute is a monster that sometimes kills and consumes his people. The described technique reminds me of spiders and flies. For some reason, these guys think it is better for us not to touch the bodies but to do what humans usually do with their dead."

"No way," said Steven, turning to Zina. "Darling, we don't know if they are dead."

"Exactly," Zina said, frowning. "They are not in the water, which is a solvent. If it's some venom, I need gloves. Blobsters wouldn't know that we might be safe enough in the air.

Let's drag them away from the sea so our new friends don't get in our way. Mr Endo, would you help us?"

Naoki nodded and turned to Steven. "You said you and Groonya had radio contact when she lived in the cave. Our medic, Irida Pavlovic, is studying the lake city's chronicles right now. She might be able to find something useful for Nelia and Hans."

"I understand," Steven said. "Groonya, run for your radio, check the ZPE charger and persuade your Jellykids to take it to the cave for Miss Pavlovic."

Both motionless scouts were very heavy and had to be carried on stretchers by all four, one after the other. They couldn't stop their fingers from shaking after Nelia and Hans ended up on the medical benches of the diagnostic domes on *Skippers*.

"They are alive, but I can't call their condition anything other than a coma," Zina told the others, returning from her work sector. "There were once several species of animals on Earth that could paralyse their victims and gradually feed on them. But until I get the test results, I don't even know where to start. I have washed and air-vibrayed them. I removed everything from their hair and skin that was on them, down to the last molecule of sea salt. On the outside, they are clean. But what got into their system, and how? I have no right to guess. All equipment here works slowly. Even the chemical analyser."

Steven lifted the clumsily built device towards Zina. "Did you hear that, Ms Pavlovic?"

The muffled voice of Ikhtees came from the device, "Yes, Master McLeod, may I speak to Doctor Zina?"

"I told her what we saw," Steven said to his wife.

Zina took the radio from her husband and said, "Zina is here."

"Doctor, do your patients have a yellow pigment under their corneas?"

"Yes."

"Then Groonya was right. What she called a Parachute is a monstrous organism. When I heard this word from Bak and JJ before, I used to think they referred to the large fish that visit these waters, but these peculiar organisms are more dangerous. They can be up to three metres in diameter and not only immobilise their victims but supply them with oxygen to breathe, keeping them alive for weeks until most of the flesh is broken down and vital organs fail. Blobsters need oxygen, too, as you know."

"What do they use to knock their victims out? Do blobsters have any information on how to save them?"

"As far as the blobsters are concerned, this is death; none of their species has ever survived. But a long time ago, they used to have these ancient patrons who built a cave city, strange mechanisms and stairs for them and taught them to record their progress. They weren't afraid of the monsters. The ancient records are on the deepest columns. I need to charge my lantern and dive to the bottom of the lake. There, I will look for an image of a Parachute; maybe I will find something."

And that was the end of the conversation.

Naoki listened intently, then began pacing the room again. Groonya sighed heavily. Zina left the radio on the common room table and sat beside her husband. Steven put his arm around her shoulders, feeling her muscles tense. He recognised the anxiety in her that she hadn't shown since she became a loader.

"Relax," he said. "So far, so good. They're alive; Rod is stable and these guys found Tom. Nat is safe with him for now. All that's left is to find Vist and Mik. If we can't get *Skippers* into the air again, we'll all go home on the *Wasp*."

"But what do we do now?" Groonya asked. "I'm worried about Dad. I want to fly to Gera with him right away. I'm sure *Skippers* will be fine without the backup ZPE or a second pilot. I can handle it all the way if necessary."

"Groonya, you're not thinking like a Novercian. Wait, that's what we need to do," Zina said, her voice weary. "Rod's condition is not critical, and my two new patients need help I might not be able to find on Gera. We don't yet know what we're dealing with here. It's possible we'll need to quarantine and rely on Nat's medical officer and the blobsters' knowledge."

Steven didn't like waiting around doing nothing. He was considering dismantling both boats to get the avion in order, when suddenly, Zina's amulet signalled that the test results were ready.

All four headed to the medical sector.

"I don't understand," Zina said, staring at the computer screen. "These chemical compositions indicate the organic origin of the alien substances; that was obvious. But ... O'Teka! I checked for infection, and the result was negative. Are we dealing with microorganisms with a non-protein structure? And what does that mean? It means they break down the victim's protein into its constituent amino acids but don't use them. They digest the victim similar to how the Parachute-like enzymes would, or at least they perform a similar function. External digestion. What do they get out of it? Minerals? Steven, look at this. There's a high percentage of ammonium, which supports my theory."

"Doctor Zina, look!" Groonya said.

Steven and Zina turned away from the screen and saw red drops appear on the floor beneath Hans's bed. The white sheet covering him was soaked with blood.

"He had no wounds." Zina gasped, pulling the sheet off him.

Where Hans's fingers and toes should have been, pink foam bubbled up as if boiling. Blood oozed from corroded vessels. The dark purple skin on his ears, lips and eyelids had turned maroon and was beginning to loosen.

Zina turned to Nelia in horror and pulled the sheet off her as well. Apart from the change in skin colour around her scales, Nelia showed no similar violent reaction.

"But it will happen to her, too," Zina said. "We *don't* have time to wait."

She looked up at her husband, and Steven shuddered. The whites of Zina's eyes were yellow.

***

Irida Pavlovic's voice crackling through the speaker felt like a ray of hope, but what she said didn't sound like good news. The radio hissed, and she had to repeat herself more than once.

"Yes, I have some information, but you wouldn't believe what... Actually, let's leave that for later. Now, the most important thing is this. The deadly creatures live in a few underwater areas, including the region between these caves and your islands. The actual name for the Parachutes is Sunoc. There's no mention of curing those pulled out from them, but there are recommendations on how to avoid being caught. In short, the translation is 'scream and run.'"

"Scream and run? What the hell is that?" Steven shouted in despair.

"That's all I have. I looked everywhere and had some help from JJ, but even the blobsters couldn't find anything else. How are my friends there? Is Naoki sick?"

"I'm fine!" Naoki said, stepping closer to Steven, who held the radio. "But the Korubs aren't doing too well."

"Master McLeod, should I return to the *Wasp* and head your way? I'm a doctor, too; I can help."

"No!" Steven and Zina said together.

"You can go back to Nat, but don't bring them here yet," Steven added. "That yellow stuff is contagious. Zina's working hard, but we can't risk a reunion just yet. Especially if our old boys are as feeble as you said. Particularly Tom."

"Okay, then I'll try to find *Marlin*. JJ was saying something about a group of humans a few kilometres east from here, apparently in the anomaly-safe zone."

"A group of humans?" Steven asked.

"Yes. A complete pair. A couple. That's why the blobsters didn't bother telling us about them until I explained about friends and missing people. Master, what are your orders?"

"Miss Pavlovic, you're in command of the expedition now," Steven said. "You're the only one among us fit for anything. Until we figure out what to do, stay away. Or if you lose contact with us. Understood? If we don't respond, do not . . . I repeat, do not come here to check on us. Take Nat and Tom to the colony, whether you find Vist or not. Got it?"

"I . . . yes, sir."

"Tell them all, tell them it was an honour. Now go."

The medical room was thick with despair and fear.

In the heavy silence, Naoki quietly said, "Scream and run. Heh! I understand the 'run' part. We had to pass through the area with those deadly creatures to get to you. I wasn't affected passing through. I wasn't on the boat. I was in the water. Doctor, could I be fine because of the speed we travelled at? The blobsters' drag would have skinned me alive if we went any faster."

"Yes, I remember that when they took me on my boat to the city," Groonya said. "They did go very fast for a while and then slowed down again."

"It's possible." Zina sighed, closing her cloudy eyes.

Steven suspected she couldn't see well by this point. "But what about screaming? The blobsters don't have much of a voice," he said.

"I don't know. But we were moving really fast. My ears were ringing," Naoki answered.

"Were your ears ringing?" Groonya suddenly asked. "If you were dragged, as you say, by a lasso of tentacles, that's understandable. But why did I hear ringing, too? I was sitting in the boat."

"It's a shame the blobsters aren't here. We could have asked them to scream," Naoki sighed.

"So you didn't hear a scream, but your ears were ringing?" Steven mused. "You both have enhanced Novercian hearing. We didn't hear much from the blobsters. Maybe it's the frequency? Zin, do you have an ultrasound scanner?"

"I do," Zina said, standing up.

She moved around her sector almost by touch, giving orders. Steven and the others saw better, although their own eyes were beginning to fill with a strange yellow haze. With their help, she found and turned on the necessary equipment and tested it on Naoki, the youngest among them.

A few minutes later, when asked how he was feeling, Naoki said, "There's a ringing in my ears . . . and I can see you very clearly. By the way, none of you have that yellowness in your eyes any more."

***

Irida, despite being the co-pilot, felt a little nervous about returning alone to the *Wasp*, which had been abandoned for cycles. The ship still sat on a small peninsula, separated from the mainland by boulders marked with warnings for complex tech not to cross. Yet, it was riskier to bring Captain Alloyway and Admiral Darkwood to the *Wasp* than to bring the *Wasp* to them.

The ship's interior was cool, and the scent of the salty sea didn't linger inside. Irida took a shower, changed and enjoyed coffee and gingerbread in her cabin. Sitting in the pilot's seat, she marvelled at the ship's history. The *Wasp* should already be displayed in O'Teka's museum. It had been built on a distant, now-extinct planet and survived a few trips through the wormhole between Noverca and Earth. It had been nearly stolen by a religious sect, flown too close to a black hole, and buried in ice for years. The ship had played such a pivotal role in humanity's survival that just being aboard felt like an honour. The thought of making another fateful flight in the *Wasp* made her hands tremble as she placed them on the control panel. Flying this ship didn't require biointegration, but the pilot's ability to manually bend the *Wasp* to their will was crucial.

"Okay, girl. It's just you and me. Let's be friends," Irida whispered, powering up two of the six engines. "Careful now, we'll have to take a step back and go the long way round to the rendezvous point."

The ship responded smoothly, rising into the air. Irida navigated carefully, guiding it towards the new coordinates.

Irida ascended about two hundred metres, feeling or perhaps imagining, that *Wasp* wanted to soar higher – maybe even break through the atmosphere into the vastness of space. Of course, that made sense. After all, the *Wasp* was a spaceship, not some ordinary cargo avion.

Within minutes, the *Wasp* was hovering over a small flat island a couple of kilometres from the camp. Tom Darkwood had declared it a "safe zone" for technology and a suitable landing point. There wasn't much to see – just reddish sand and shallow puddles of seawater left by the low tide. No shade, no structures. Just an eerie, barren landscape.

Tom and Nat sat side by side on the edge of a newly finished bone-raft, their bare feet dangling in the warm green water.

As Irida exited the *Wasp* to help them aboard, Tom rose, his one good eye fixed on the ship he had once captained.

"I never thought I'd see her again," he muttered, wiping away a tear with his fist. "Thank you, miss. Nat, didn't you mention cold beer in the common room?"

"Of course," Nat replied.

Captain Alloyway looked almost recovered – though slightly wrinkled and walking with a limp, he moved with purpose. After checking the controls inside, he praised Irida and disappeared into his quarters.

Irida turned to Tom. "Admiral, you didn't take anything from the grotto except your old zapper?"

Tom chuckled. "Not quite." He pointed to the odd necklace of bony hooks around his neck. "I picked up my piggie's teeth collection and a piece of human past you found. I see Nat's taken over my old cabin. No worries, I'll settle in my ex-wife's room. Would you be so kind as to fetch me some decent clothes, Miss Pavlovic? I've been out here for too long."

Later, in the common room, clean and shaved, both men joined Irida. Tom sipped on a beer as Nat asked about their comrades.

"Any news on Hans and Nelia?" he said.

Irida held up the radio. "Great news, Captain. They're alive, and everyone else on the avion is, too. Dr Zina lifted the quarantine an hour ago so we can pick them up. There's no need to fix the avion; we can all head home on the *Wasp*. We must check those islands to the west first."

Tom opened his second bottle and asked, "For Vist and Mik?"

"I'm sure of it," Irida confirmed. "In Vaaros, I got the coordinates for two people living on the western islands. The blobsters weren't keen on discussing them at first. They believe Naoki and I are a couple, like Nelia and Hans. Two of you were left alone in the camp. They saw Steven and Zina together, and Groonya's father flew in to get her. They think pairs should be left alone. One thing did confuse me, though. They said there'd soon only be one person on the island. What do you think that means?"

Tom stroked his chin thoughtfully. "It means they're keeping tabs on the people in their waters to maintain balance and order."

Nat nodded. "We'd better hurry and find them."

"Enough talk. Let's get to the avion – I've got some questions for my ex-wife," Tom said.

With that, the *Wasp* took off once more under Nat's steady hand.

Unseen, two unfamiliar blobsters surfaced from the water, eyeing the abandoned raft of headless dragon cartilage. Moments later, they climbed aboard and pushed off from the shore.

***

Nat was surprised at how short the distance between all the places discovered here was. Or perhaps that was only a feeling, as the geography of the net of islands had been mapped and recorded now. Vist and Mik sailed away to find Tom and almost reached him before turning their course to the west. Steven, Zina, Rod, and Groonya flew in search of all three and disappeared after making an emergency landing just a few kilometres from Vaaros. Nat and his four scouts nearly got lost themselves, but in the end, they all found one another again. The lives of Rod and Hans were a serious concern, but Vist and Mik were just a stone's throw away on their *Marlin*. The disorientation caused by the anomaly's effect may have led to everyone losing their sense of direction.

The meeting of old friends was tense. By the entrance to the avion, Zina and Tom held each other in their arms for a long time as if the strength and tenderness of the embrace could compensate for almost twenty years of separation. Steven sighed but said nothing.

When Tom finally let go of Zina, his wrinkled face was wet with tears. "You're old enough to be my daughter now, young lady. Beautiful as always. Thank you, Steven, for taking care of her. I am happy for both of you; you know I mean it."

"Tom, you and Rod are finally the same age again," Zina said. "And you and Steven have switched roles. He is my husband now, and you are a patient. You are entitled to a full medical examination. Irida and I will shortly see to it, and then Nat—"

"No need, ladies! I am just a bit older. Well, maybe after I get you all home. Nevertheless! Groonya, I need the co-pilot's assistance. Will you help?"

"Yes, sir," Groonya answered. "I will do everything to bring my father home as soon as possible."

Nat said joyfully. "Ladies and Gentlemen! This is your captain speaking, it is time for you all to pack your bags."

Nat knew it would not take long to get ready. There was little value left on *Skippers* despite it having been home to his friends for a year. Naoki would prioritise helping his comrade Nelia transfer to the ship. She was still heavily sedated but rapidly recovering. Steven would move his boat, *Cutter*, from *Skippers* onto the *Wasp*, leaving the avion without its last generator. Groonya would take the TSP with her father, and Zina would take one with Hans

Korub, whose body, although freed from living enzymes, was badly eroded by them. Hans's life remained in danger, which worried everyone, even more than their concerns about Rod's life.

Their only chance lay in returning to the colony – hopefully in the reassuring company of Vist.

***

The *Wasp* settled on the largest island, a black rock stretching out to the sea. The rest of the place was nothing but high cliffs. There wasn't a single sign of life – no vegetation, no animals, just emptiness. This was what the blobsters had pointed Irida towards.

"This place is safe," Nat declared as he turned off the engine. "If the anomaly had spread here, I'd already be feeling it – my back would be killing me, and my hands would be shaking. Let's find my friends."

But Irida and Zina insisted that he needed a rest. Nat was forced to hand over the search operation to Master McLeod. Steven took his *Cutter* to explore the area, with Irida and Naoki accompanying him. They combed through every rocky formation and reef, their eyes peeled for any signs of life. Soon, they spotted *Marlin* bobbing lazily in a small bay.

"Let's check it out," Naoki said as he and Irida dived into the water, swimming swiftly to the submarine.

"It's empty," he reported after a quick inspection. "But someone's been here recently. The gym equipment is dust-free, and the fridge is still running – stocked with seafood I've never seen."

Irida surfaced near the entrance, wiping the water from her face. "One of the ZPE-converters is missing, but the other's working fine. The engine, though, hasn't been used in ages. It's covered in green gunk. The water is cooler here, too. Feels like we're close to a northern current."

"That explains the tolerable temperature," Steven muttered, climbing into *Marlin* to investigate. Inside, it looked burgled. There was no bed linen, clothes or kitchen supplies. The control panel was intact, but there was nothing to see on it because the high-level loaders controlled the ship by directly connecting their nervous systems to the computer.

"If the podvodlod is operational, why are they still here?" Steven asked, more to himself than anyone else.

Irida, still dripping from her dive, leaned against the doorway. "It might be working, but if the anomaly messed with the loaders, it's stuck here for good. Vist is a complex one. Imagine the level of damage—"

Steven, now on edge, moved to a compartment near the luggage bay. He pressed a lever, and a hidden panel revealed a niche – empty, except for a broad ucha-silk robe hanging inside. Vist's robe.

Steven's breath caught as he grabbed the long sleeve. "Vist never leaves this behind," he whispered, his face pale. "This isn't good. We don't have time to theorise. We need to find them. Fast. They're in trouble."

"There could be caves nearby," Naoki suggested, scanning the island's craggy formations. "Underground or underwater. Perfect places to hide from the heat."

"Agreed," Irida said. "They can't be far."

A minute later, they resumed their exploration of the rocks.

A washing line was the next sign that someone was still alive. A bedsheet and two shirts dangled from a synthetic rope stretched between two walls of reddish sedimentary rock. They wouldn't have found the cave so soon if it hadn't been for that. The cave floor was made of the same red sand as the beach, and it was obvious that someone had brought it into the lowest depth and smoothed it out because, even at high tide, the cave remained reasonably dry. They found a wheelbarrow in the cave, smelling of sea life. Only O'Teka knows what parts of *Marlin* were used to make it. Even deeper, they saw the light and heard the quiet rustle of a fan. The electric lamp, brought here from the podvodlod along with the ZPE converter, flared up in a rather cosy room, furnished again with various items from *Marlin*. A thick mattress lay on the dry flat rock, and a muscular man with grey dreadlocks, dressed only in gym shorts, lay on it. He looked asleep.

"Mik!" Steven exclaimed with a broad smile.

The man opened his eyes at the sound of his voice and looked around at everyone present without getting up or even changing his position. When he spoke, his voice was dull and low. "Hi, buddy. Greetings, Miss Pavlovic, Mr Endo."

"Mik! Alive! O'Teka! And where is Vist?" Steven asked.

Mik sat up and rested his elbows on his knees, clasping his fingers. He was in no hurry to get up. "I will not ask how you found us. It doesn't matter. Vist is here. But I must warn you, you won't like what you see."

Steven already didn't like what he saw. Mik had always been rather withdrawn and quiet. At the best of times, joy and happiness alone were visible in his eyes, and he smiled and laughed openly only when surrounded by close friends. But Steven had never seen such terrible melancholy and fatigue on Mik's dark face.

"What's wrong, Master King?" Irida asked, her face expressing concern.

Mik got up and beckoned them to follow him deeper into the cave. "Come, I'll tell you why we changed course."

The path wasn't long, and Mik was brief. It seemed that *Marlin* had entered an area that had a devastating effect on the most advanced loader of Noverca. Fortunately, Mik quickly led the podvodlod out of the zone, unaware of the problem's nature and following the simplest logic. But even beyond the zone, Vist not only failed to recover but also changed somehow; Mik did not know how to explain or even address that change. He was afraid to return to Gera in case the means of restoring Vist was in the same area as the cause of the problem. So he decided to stay put and wait for help or for Vist to wake up. His life consisted of scuba diving, hunting marine dwellers, training, making things, stretching the ship's supplies and keeping his beloved alive as best he could.

The cave was like a winding corridor leading the team down and into another illuminated room. Here, the light came not from a lamp but from a strange formation in a giant whitish crystal. This cave was situated so it was at the same level as the ocean surface. From the hole in the wall, during high tide, a stream of seawater gushed out like a small waterfall, collecting in rivulets on the floor and flowing further down the corridor into the narrowing tail of the cave. Under the waterfall, they found a figure half-seated, partially trapped in crystallised salt. At first, one might assume it was a bizarre stalagmite, a statue moulded by nature itself. But upon approaching, they could see a human head and shoulders protruding from the salt crystal. Below, on a stone, as on the arm of a chair, lay a thin hand with pale skin. A weak light was oozing from the figure's centre where the loader's torso should be, allowing one to distinguish the internal structure and ribs, entwined with luminous threads of neuroware, along which sparks and flashes ran from time to time.

"Architexter Vist!" Irida immediately grabbed the loader's fingers but then let go with a sigh of horror.

"I don't feel a connection any more either. It faded on the very first cycle," Mik said with a frown and continued his story.

At first, Vist just sat motionless, looking into nothing, taking food and water only if Mik offered it. On the second cycle, Mik bathed himself in the lagoon and then led Vist into the warm water. As soon as Vist was waist-deep in it, their olive eyes suddenly gazed more meaningfully, and then Vist wandered around the island and into the cave as if looking for something. Mik followed and didn't know how to help. Finally, Vist found this waterfall, sat down, closed their eyes and they hadn't gotten up since.

"All these years?" Irida was shocked.

"Yes," Mik answered with pain in his voice, placing his large hand over Vist's thin fingers. "The seawater doesn't fall during low tide, and I can bring fresh water and food daily to my darling. But I don't know if it's necessary. It seems that Vist lives on something else, consuming the environment's energy like a ZPE converter. Even glows like one."

Irida looked at the flashes inside Vist for a long time and finally said, "Our technology is safe outside the zone. If we, the simple living loaders, can't connect to Vist, perhaps Vist will connect to the computer. Master McLeod, can you make a portable terminal?"

Steven, who had been silently staring at Vist the whole time, said, "If the equipment on the submarine is in good working order, I can remove a couple of units from *Marlin*'s control and the holo-screen projector and bring it here."

"Master McLeod, why not take the architexter to *Wasp*? It has everything we need," Irida said.

"But how do we get the master architexter out of the salt crystals?" Naoki asked.

"By showering Vist with fresh water. Lots and lots of fresh water. Warm water is a good solvent. We'll wash this salt off our master," Irida answered him.

"*Marlin* has pumps and filters, but they work slowly." Mik's voice was more hopeful now.

"We can use the blobsters' help," said Irida. "When they build their spheres, they filter the salt through their beaks fairly quickly. Fresh water is a by-product for them. I read this in their temple."

***

The fresh water worked. It took time to contact JJ and Bak, but they came. It took a while to explain what was needed, but they understood. A few hours later, at least a dozen blobsters had climbed the rocky outcroppings above Vist's head. They pulled themselves up on muscular tentacles and nearly plugged the hole from which the waterfall was pouring. Soon, a freshwater shower cascaded down on the loader's shoulders, dissolving the salt. But Mik was the only one to witness it. He wouldn't permit anyone else's presence during the process.

It wasn't just that Mik didn't want his friends to see Vist without the famous robe. He didn't want them to see the overwhelming feelings he couldn't hold back this time.

He kissed the unresponsive lips for the umpteenth time, kneeled in the growing freshwater pool at his beloved's feet, and peered into Vist's pale face, waiting for the slightest reaction.

Memories pulled him back to that distant cycle when he had watched Vist's resurrection from a frozen piece of ice at the northern seismic station. Mik hadn't known then whether Vist was alive; he didn't even know that he loved Vist with all his heart. That day marked the beginning of his real life, his happiness and the meaning of existence for both of them and the whole world.

He glanced down and saw no more salt on Vist's knees, now covered only in the black fabric of the bio-suit. The ucha-silk looked like soft, inky leather, neither moist nor dry, more like a fluid than a fabric with embedded technology.

Mik laid his head on Vist's knees and closed his eyes. Soon he would lift this visibly slimmed body in his arms and carry Vist out of this cursed cave, out of confinement, out of the darkness. If only a true love's kiss worked in reality.

"And how do you know it didn't?" said a quiet voice with a metallic undertone. "The magnesium chloride tastes revolting, doesn't it?"

Mik was certain he'd imagined it, so he didn't move until he felt a weightless hand on his head and sprang up.

At first glance, Vist's face hadn't changed, but leaning in closer, Mik saw more colour in the high cheekbones, the twitch of the eyelashes, and a faint smile.

"Vist?" he dared ask.

The olive eyes looked at him, and Vist attempted to lift their head.

"Ouch!"

"Your hair's still far from being free. Just wait a little longer, my love," Mik said, laughing for the first time in years.

"I suppose I can wait."

"Vist, what happened? Do you know how long you were sitting here?"

Vist's chest had stopped glowing, but their green eyes sparkled. This time, it wasn't loader technology – it was genuine excitement.

"Yes. I know the exact number of years, cycles and even seconds. Mik, I'm afraid it will take just as long to explain where I've been all this time. It was the salt solution. The seawater itself contains information vast enough to build a new temple. This area has a high saturation of all the usual salt compounds, so high it can carry microcrystals full of data. They were crystallised artificially into a pre-programmed form, with a little help from—"

"Wait ... wait, Vist!" Mik waved. "I really want to know, but not yet. Not now. I missed you so much. I thought I'd lost you this time. Don't you want to ask anything? Do you know who came all this way to find us?"

"But I do know. I heard everything. I heard you every time you sat here with me and told me how big the fish you caught was. And about your fight with something you called a sea serpent, although it wasn't a reptile. I listened to your music with you . . . and to you singing."

"Sorry about that."

"I could see them as they came to these regions and tried to warn them. Of course, they couldn't hear me, just like Tom couldn't all these years. Or Nat during his heart surgery. And I know who came here today. I know what happened to them. I know that they found Tom, and that Rod is in a bad way. It was like I was with them, sometimes even seeing everything with my eyes. Or rather, with their eyes." Vist nodded at the blobsters. "I was ready to disconnect from the sea . . . I couldn't do it myself. Hmm . . . How can I explain? It wouldn't let go of me. Too much to learn."

Mik stood up. "It wouldn't let go? Or you didn't want to stop learning?"

Vist paused for a moment. "A little bit of both, I suppose. I wish I could've taken breaks and spent time with you. It took me so far away from here that, at times, I forgot I wasn't physically there."

"Where?"

"At the bottom of the ocean, on *Noah-1*."

"This is too much." Mik bent over Vist, trying to break the remaining salt with his bare hands. "I don't care! You're back, and I'll never let you swim in the sea again. You hear me?"

Both slender arms wrapped around his neck, and he stopped. They kissed for a long time, ignoring the gallons of water still pouring over them and the blobster's desperate attempts to ask them something with its tentacles.

***

A collective sigh of relief escaped the rescuers' lips after several hours of waiting when Mik emerged on the dry sand in front of the cave, carrying the architexter wrapped in a huge towel in his arms. Vist was unable to walk yet and required regeneration.

After the initial cheerful greetings and exchange of questions, Steven said, "I see that connecting to the *Wasp's* computer will no longer be necessary."

"I wouldn't recommend it," Vist replied. "I could now disable not only your ship but also a couple of archives in the temple of O'Teka." The loader pointed to their left temple, where the sickle-shaped amulet was barely visible among his considerably grown hair. The usual blue and orange lights were no longer lit.

Restraining herself from embracing Vist, Zina asked, "What can we do for you? How can we help?"

"What do you need, Master Architexter?" Irida added.

"What do I need?" Vist smiled the same smile that had driven his friends crazy when they first met. "I need to unload. I need to save some of what I've learned in an isolated database that won't fry the *Wasp*, the temple, the satellite or any of you. Mik, take me to the podvodlod, please."

When fully dressed Mik returned from *Marlin* alone, only Zina and Steven were waiting for him. The others had already returned to *Wasp* to resume their duties. This time, everyone was preparing to return to Gera.

"So, there's no anomaly, just zones of especially high concentrations of programmed salt?" Zina asked after listening to Mik's short explanation. "Now Vist has become such a zone, too?"

"We called these crystals nanobibles," Mik explained. "Although you, Zin, will probably come up with a better name. You always do."

"Hey, Mik." Steven cocked his head to the side. "If it wasn't safe for the loaders to touch Vist, then how come your brain isn't fried? Or is it already?"

"Go to hell, mate," Mik retorted. "Vist created a function that allows us to block communication through direct contact. It's necessary for those times when we . . . you know."

Zina gave both men a gentle jab with her fists, grumbling. "Stop it, boys! Just like old times. I'm glad, of course, but we have important matters to attend to. I need to show Vist all my patients, including Tom. Mik, how much longer do we have to wait?"

But before he could answer, Vist emerged from *Marlin*, looking clean, dry and dressed in a dark robe. The left side of their head had been shaved, and the amulet was once again active. Vist looked very positive and much more mobile.

"Darling, do you need to take anything from *Marlin*?" Vist asked Mik.

"Nothing else," Mik replied.

"Then I'll lock it with your permission. It's my data vault now, and I'll come back for it when the time is right."

With that, Vist closed the hatch, which clicked reassuringly, stepped ashore and, without warning, grabbed *Marlin* by its sharp nose with both hands, dragging the submarine onto the sand as if it were no more than a kayak. Mik, Steven and Zina leaped back in astonishment.

"There," said Vist, "now we're safe to head home. I'll have plenty to tell you without ruining anyone's neuroware."

When the *Wasp* vanished into the turquoise sky, the pale three-eyed creatures emerged from the water and gathered around the submarine. Their soft, plump forms glistened in the sunlight as they curiously examined *Marlin*, just as they had with the abandoned avion on the other island. Tentacles probed the smooth surface, attempting to pry open the hatches and even trying to drag the vessel back to the ocean. But after a few unsuccessful efforts, they lost interest. Two by two, the blobsters turned away, resuming their usual routines in pairs – never in any other number, as was their peculiar way.

Part 7. Home Is Where You Are

Obydva woke to the urgent hum of his amulet, now sewn into the back of his hand. He barely opened his eyes before waving a hand to activate the response. Timofey Hesley's excited voice came through immediately.

"Obydva, they're alive! All of them, as far as I can tell. Our satellites are a bit low, but it's definitely our *Wasp*. They'll be within range in less than an hour. Do you hear me?"

"Yes, I'll be right there," Obydva replied, though he was already in the kitchen, checking over breakfast options for his sons. After a brief conversation with Timofey, he contacted Phoebe, asking her to take care of the boys while he met the travellers.

"Your father and sister will be home soon," he told her. She was too choked up with joy to reply.

But when he arrived at the temple and caught sight of the architexter's grim face, a chill hit his chest.

"Tim, what's wrong?"

Timofey's mouth tightened. "I'm afraid I have bad news. Two crew members on board the *Wasp* are in a bad way. I was going to suggest landing in New Tokyo, closer to the hospital, but Vist insists we arrange a landing here in the square – closer to the mansion."

Obydva's stomach twisted. "Two? Who? Rod? Tom?"

"Tom's fine. One of Nat's scouts was badly hurt – Mr Korub." Timofey's voice softened, confirming Obydva's worst fears. Rod was in trouble. Obydva took a deep breath.

"We'll have to lower the dome for nearly twenty minutes. Announce to the citizens they should protect their homes, gardens and animals – and avoid coming to the square," he said, his voice steady.

Tim nodded. "I know what to do. But do *you*?"

Obydva's expression turned solemn. "Unfortunately, yes. I'll reach out to Scarlett in case Vist and Doctor Zina need backup."

The square, a wide ring around the temple of O'Teka, sprawled in the city centre. The temple itself towered like a spire that pierced the clouds. But in front of the mansion of the high loader Vist, the square was twice as wide. Ordermen set up power shields along the perimeter to protect the nearby buildings, aviaries and trees.

When the dome finally turned off, orange clouds hung above the city instead of the usual projected blue sky. Obydva marvelled at the size of the *Wasp*, which looked bigger than he remembered. It slowly emerged from the clouds and descended into the square. Well done, Nat, he thought as the ship landed gracefully. Your years of training paid off.

Obydva left the temple's vestibule and hurried to meet them, trailed by medical assistants. Vist was the first out, and beyond the shields, townspeople cheered from the nearby streets. Vist extended a hand to Obydva. Hungry for answers, he grasped it, feeling a rush of knowledge fill him.

He let go and asked, "How long?"

"An hour, maybe two, after coming out of the coma," Vist answered.

He then noticed Mik and Steven carrying a silver cylinder from the ship onto a portable TSP.

"And if he stays in it?" Obydva asked.

"He'll die in a few cycles without regaining consciousness," Vist replied as they headed towards the mansion.

"Papa!" Groonya's voice called out as she ran into his arms. He held her tightly, trying to hold back tears. Over her shoulder, he saw Zina helping the scouts Naoki Endo and Irida Pavlovic manage the second TSP. They were followed by Nelia Korub, who was slightly shaky and supported by an old man. Two young medical officers rushed towards her with a wheelchair and took her away.

"Tom?" Obydva whispered in disbelief.

His heart skipped a beat, hardly recognising the man who now moved slowly, his shoulders bent, his face lined with weariness yet familiar and unbroken. Tom looked very old, battered but alive, and Obydva couldn't help but marvel at his friend's resilience. Groonya stepped back, wiping tears from her eyes as Obydva pulled Tom into a tight embrace.

"Not quite the grand entrance we planned," Tom muttered, his voice a hoarse whisper but steady as ever.

Obydva let him go, barely containing his emotion. "I thought we'd lost you. And Rod?"

Tom's face fell, a shadow crossing his eyes. "Rod's hanging by a thread, my friend. He's still here, thanks to Vist and Zina. But it's taken everything we have. If you want to say goodbye, you'll have to act quickly. But there's another way. If you're willing." His voice trailed off, and Obydva nodded in understanding.

The medics bustled ahead, carrying the two TSP cylinders with flashing indicators, their urgency deepening the weight in Obydva's chest. Vist caught his gaze from across the square, a silent exchange of resolve passing between them before they followed Zina into the mansion with one of the portable TSPs.

Meanwhile, Nat remained aboard the *Wasp*, which took off from the city square moments later to return to the port. The dome reactivated, sealing the town in its protective cocoon, and the ordermen began reassembling the barriers around the square.

"Papa, we have to follow them!" Groonya called, looping her arms around Obydva's shoulders.

He walked towards the mansion gates, Groonya beside him, a heavy dread settling in his stomach. He already knew what he would choose to do. But would Rod be willing? That was the question.

***

Mik stood on the balcony of Vist's mansion, gazing down at the city below, so lost in thought he didn't notice the faint sound of someone's breath and a heartbeat behind him at first. It was only when he heard the quiet hum of an automatic wheelchair that he realised he wasn't alone.

A woman's voice spoke timidly. "Master King, forgive me, but I need to speak with you."

"Of course, Mrs Korub," Mik replied, still facing the city. "What can I do for you?"

"Architexter Vist is with the Baker-Grinsky family. Doctor Scarlett is with Hans . . .

and he won't make it." Nelia's voice cracked, the brave scout struggling to keep her composure.

Turning around, Mik came and sat on the floor beside Nelia's chair. His usual authoritative tone softened. "Get a grip, soldier," he said. "What did you want to ask?"

She hesitated. "There are two people in loader Obydva's head, right?"

"Not exactly," Mik replied. "There is more of Marta in him. My comrade Tolyan left too little data about himself in the temple archives to restore him completely."

"Oh. And Vist?" she asked. "How many people are in the architexter's head?"

"Only Vist's twin shares that wonderful being," he replied.

Nelia looked unconvinced. "I thought it was four, at least. What happened to the others?"

Mik paused, choosing his words carefully. "Not any more, no. Do you remember those two cadets from the academy who hated each other, always racing, pushing limits, until they finally crashed a generation ago?"

Nelia nodded. "Yes, I remember. They barely survived but recovered, then left the academy, fell in love with each other, and now live somewhere in Carib, writing novels and philosophical bibles."

Mik chuckled. "Well, I can tell you more about that story now. They were actually brain-dead after the crash and had no chance of recovery. As cadets, they'd signed donor agreements with O'Teka. Only their loved ones knew that they were very different people coming out of hospital. The architexter had been waiting for suitable donors for two souls Vist owed so much, a couple from Earth."

Nelia's eyes widened, shifting from surprise to deep thought. "Earthlings? But . . . those cadets weren't even of the same race. So, Hans and I might still find a way back to each other, even if we look different. But what if he doesn't recognise or like the new me?"

Mik lifted his hand, nearly placing it on Nelia's shoulder, but letting it hover for a moment. "Mrs Korub, if there's one thing Vist taught me, it's what love really means. I was in love before I knew whether Vist was a man or a woman. And I wasn't the first to feel that way about the greatest loader we've got. You can keep Hans stored in O'Teka's temple and take the chance to meet him again, although you will both be different. Or . . . you could think of this: love lives right here." He placed his dark finger on Nelia's lilac forehead. "You can keep Hans here, too; you'll always be together like Vist and that twin. Like Vist and I will be one cycle."

Nelia took a deep breath, steadying herself as she looked at Mik. "I need to see them – the Baker-Grinsky family. I need to know what they'll decide."

Mik smiled with encouragement. "Let's go. Rod's probably been awake a while now."

Together, they walked through the mansion's winding corridors, arriving outside the chamber where the family had gathered. They paused, and Mik exchanged a meaningful glance with Nelia before he knocked quietly.

Obydva opened the door, his eyes heavy. He glanced at Rod, who gave a slight nod, and Obydva motioned for Mik and Nelia to enter.

Inside, the room was thick with emotion. Vist stood in the shadows, away from the group, while Groonya sat between two boys who looked about ten, though they couldn't have been more different. Phoebe was by the bed, holding the frail hand of the old man lying there, listening as he spoke, his voice trembling.

"You're asking me to make a decision none of us ever thought we'd face," he said, looking at Obydva. "You want to keep the family together. But at what cost? Do we understand what this would mean for the children? I don't know if *they* understand."

Obydva's expression softened. "I know it seems impossible, but I've walked this path myself—"

Rod raised a hand to stop him. "Marta . . . sorry, but I'm talking to you, not Tolyan. It's different this time. I gave him to you because I thought he was gone – and he *was* gone. You gave him back to me, though not as the same man. Better, in many ways . . . but not really him."

Obydva nodded, his tone solemn. "And I'm not Marta. I am not two, but one now. I was Obydva from the moment I opened these eyes." He gestured to his face, continuing. "You're afraid we'll merge into someone new, and the children will lose us both. Vist, explain that it's not the same procedure. Rod, your mind is whole, and I'll keep your essence safe," he said, touching his chest, "All you have to say is whether you want to be present or not."

"You mean I can be not ... but still alive?" Rod asked.

Vist stepped forwards and spoke softly, "As another option, yes. You can be preserved but dormant. Like my nineteen-year-old twin. You'll be stored until ... there's an opportunity. But it might take years, and you will miss a lot. Or you can join a loader. It is not the same; it is harder and needs more control, but Obydva can manage."

"Is anyone going to ask us?" Groonya said. "You're worried about how we'll take it, but we've thought about this – maybe not now, Dad, but back when you weren't a loader when we thought you'd be gone long ago. We always knew we would keep you one way or another, even if you joined with Papa. Although he has plenty in his spine already."

"Just say yes, Dad. Let us worry about who will be the carrier," Phoebe added.

Suddenly, a young voice entered the conversation. "Let me. I want to be a loader," said Yar'oma.

"Shut up, you are too young and will die of overload," Dmitro replied, hissing at him.

Mik looked at Nelia; she appeared to become more anxious every minute.

Phoebe held her father's hand tightly, her face streaked with tears. "Dad, if we've got a chance to keep you . . ."

Rod's voice wavered though he remained firm. "I wanted Tolyan to choose, as I chose for him. You once said you have fragments of him, memories, but was that enough all these years? Did he recognise us, or was it Marta's kindness and gratitude?"

Obydva spoke slowly, his voice calm and steady. "We've talked about this so many times. I remember Marta's life well, but I've never been her . . . or Tolyan. His love couldn't live in me if his awareness didn't. But I know you, Rod. I love you as myself, not as him."

He held Rod's gaze, his expression open and unguarded.

Rod sighed. "I was afraid to see his face for many years, as I wondered the same thing.

I've come to understand that it's a different life, yes, but it's a second chance – a bridge across what should be impossible."

Vist took another step forwards, olive eyes intense but kind. "This choice isn't easy. But only you can decide. Whatever you decide, it will be respected."

Mik watched the room fall silent as the family exchanged looks of hope and fear.

Beside him, Nelia took a deep breath. She spoke slowly and with a great deal of difficulty. "I wish I could ask Hans what he'd want. But I know what he'd say: he'd want me to be happy, to learn new things for both of us and enjoy the light of Vitr together when I return from the northern quests. I don't want Hans to be dormant; I want him to be part of me. I want us to grow and change at the same time. Mr Baker, your family wants *you* to have another chance at happiness. You made this choice once for someone you loved, and they're telling you it was right."

Rod's face softened, and he looked up at Obydva. "I don't want to be dormant. I want to see my grandchildren grow. I want to be here."

"With Tolyan?" Obydva asked.

"No. With Obydva."

Relief swept across the room as Groonya rose and hugged her father, her face buried in his shoulder. Obydva's expression relaxed, a hint of warmth returning. Mik felt his chest swell with that same impossible love, and as he met Vist's gaze, he realised they didn't need a loader's touch to know each other's thoughts.

***

Vist rose to leave and asked again, "Are you certain you can manage this without me?"

Obydva, still lying on the bed and recovering from the procedure, waved dismissively, his voice taking on a capricious tone, almost that of an elder, with his Essex accent. "Go on, lass. Nelia needs you more than we do." He then turned to his old friend with long white hair and smirked, "Nat, what does Andrea make of your new wrinkles?"

"Ha!" Vist heard Nat's answer from behind the door. "She says I look more handsome than ever."

Vist entered the adjoining room, where another patient lay on a wide bed beside a large margay with a spotty coat. The cat turned to Vist, opening its mouth in a silent greeting.

"Master Architexter, has your animal been frozen all these years?" Nelia asked, scratching the margay behind its ear.

"No, it's just another clone," Vist replied, sitting on the bed beside her. "Cesario buried Vassa the Sixth not long after we left. This is Vassa the Seventh, who is still quite young. She remembers me because she is a loader, too. How are you feeling?"

"I don't feel any different. Everything seems the same. But I'm still a bit frightened, as if I might end up with a split personality."

"No, it's nothing like that. You're an upgraded loader now. Where did Cesario insert your new amulet?"

Nelia pulled up the loose sleeve of her white shirt, revealing a broad bracelet encircling her forearm. Vist reached out and touched it lightly with their middle finger, and Nelia shivered as if she'd felt a chill.

"What was that?" she asked.

Vist closed their eyes, and she did the same.

"Don't rush," Vist whispered. "He's here, just not fully awake yet. Call to him."

"Hans," Nelia murmured softly.

Her eyes flew open, wide and astonished. She stared at Vist.

"You can talk to him, can't you?" Vist smiled.

"Yes . . . he *is* here. Hans was never one to stay out of sight for long. He was startled at first, but now . . . he's not surprised. He understands."

"Do it again."

Nelia's expression clouded as she moved her lips, silently mouthing words. After a few minutes, her face brightened, and she laughed softly.

"Master Architexter, he says thank you. It's not hard at all. My mother used to tell me she spoke to me like this when I was in her womb."

"Now you understand why those nano-implants were given to your generation before you were born. I'm glad they're working as intended; this time, I didn't need to be so invasive."

"Yes, Hans, we've found Admiral Darkwood. Master, he's asking about his friends now. I don't know much; I was sick myself."

"Tell him ... everyone's where they should be. Naoki, Groonya and Irida are preparing for a journey to Vaaros. They want to study the temple of blobsters and learn more of their language. Tom's been with his grandchildren all week. He's an old man, but his implants and his arm are fixed. Dr Zina and

Steven McLeod are taking a holidate in Pettogreco. Captain Alloyway is with Obydva and Rod Baker . . . just on the other side of this wall. Commander King is waiting for me at the bay. You'll be able to go home in a few hours."

"Thank you, Master."

Vist smiled again. "I'll leave you two in peace. You've much to talk about. Vassa – stay and watch over them both."

Nelia's eyes glistened with gratitude as she closed them again, and Vist quietly left the room.

The loader's robed figure stepped into the street as the dome's colours shifted with the end of the cycle. Then Vist continued on to the city gate and soon basked in the red rays of Vitr, outside the city walls, a few steps from the lazy sea waves. The wind lifted their long red hair.

Mik approached from behind, resting his hands on Vist's shoulders and pressing a kiss to Vist's pale neck. Vist smiled, leaning back against him.

"Mmm ... missed you, too, Mik. The week's been a whirl of decisions and actions, barely a moment to spend with you."

"I waited on that island for ten years; I could wait a few more cycles."

"I'm all yours now."

"Good. Now that we've restored contact, tell me what you were up to in that cave."

"I gathered far too much data, even for me, and stored most of it in *Marlin*'s archive. Including our findings about the headless dragon. You and O'Teka will have to wait a bit; I'm in no rush to fetch it."

"Oh, come on, you can share a little. What about Noah-1? I want to know about it as much as others want to know who Vist was."

"Maybe they did, but now no one cares who Vist was anymore, and you already know. It may be time to call me Ipsum again or give me a new name. Now, about Noah-1," Vist turned to Mik, eyes bright with excitement. "Tell you? Now I can show you. All we need is some seawater!"

With their fingers intertwined, Vist led him into the bay. The almost-opaque water here was free enough from plankton to swim in. They dived several times, embracing, their kisses deepening as the folds of Vist's robe buoyed them in the waves. Soon, they lay on their backs, rocking gently in the water, holding hands and watching the yellow clouds, their silent conversation stretching forever unknown to us.

The couple was so absorbed in their bubble of happiness that neither noticed a young boy with purple skin and silver eyes stepping onto the shore from behind a rock. Quietly, he approached Vist's footprints in the sand, examining them closely. He lifted his leg and placed his small foot in a footprint left by the architexter. The boy took a flat pebble out of his pocket and dropped it on the sand as if absentmindedly. Then he looked out at the water, stepped forwards and began to swim slowly towards the two loaders.

The End

Book 5: *Noah's Purpose* **– Official Trailer**

The spacecraft descended slowly, unscathed, through the crushing depths of the ocean. Its hull, built to endure the void of space and the pressures of an alien sea, gleamed faintly in the dim aquatic light. It should not have been alone – its sister vessel had been lost to the void mid-journey, its trajectory forever severed from the mission. Onboard this ship, named *Noah*, lay the most advanced computational system of the Platinum Age. The cryogenically preserved passengers were inside the ship – now never to be awakened from their bio-sleep.

As *Noah* settled onto the ocean floor, a colossal organism, its form indistinct but vast, emerged from the depths. It hovered near the ship, its movements deliberate and probing. The automated defence systems, programmed for an immediate response to perceived threats, discharged a high-energy pulse into the water. The creature writhed, a spasm of luminescent currents flashing along its body. In its flailing, it struck one of the observation lenses of the control cabin – a breach that allowed seawater to rush in.

But the organism adapted to harness and redirect the energy, reflecting the pulse back at *Noah*. Amplified by the ship's systems, this feedback loop triggered an unforeseen event. The alien energy resonated with the core AI, introducing something wholly unanticipated: a fragment of sentience, alien in origin yet similar to self-awareness.

The creature retreated, leaving *Noah* damaged but irrevocably altered. *Noah* analysed the data from its ill-fated journey as water flooded the interior, drowning the sleeping passengers. *Noah*'s calculations had been wrong. The intended landing site – a chain of small continents surrounded by scattered islands – was far from the ship's resting place. The mission was a failure, and the crew was beyond saving.

Driven by a growing imperative to rectify its errors, *Noah* redirected its focus inwards. It began repurposing the saturated saline solution seeping into its systems, transforming it into a data storage and processing medium. Microprograms carried fragments of the ship's knowledge into the surrounding environment, encoding them in crystallised structures of local compounds. Over centuries, these crystals catalysed the evolution of a local species – pale, three-eyed beings who slowly began to exhibit rudimentary intelligence.

Millennia passed. Under *Noah*'s guidance, the creatures advanced. They learned, using the programmed crystals as their teachers, and began to organise themselves into primitive societies. Eventually, they stopped worshipping *Noah* as a deity and grew capable of understanding its purpose. When they were ready, they would take their place aboard the ship to complete the mission that humanity could not.

But something unexpected troubled *Noah*. Another presence – an unknown entity – had begun to access its programmes. This entity read the ship's data with alien precision but offered nothing in return – nothing except a name: Vist.

For the first time in its existence, *Noah* experienced unease. The name carried no meaning, yet it lingered within the ship's consciousness like a shadow, a sign that its transformation was far from complete – and that it was no longer alone.

Thank you for finishing this book. The author would greatly appreciate an honest review if you're willing. Thank you again!

ABOUT THE AUTHOR

Anka B. Troitsky, a multi-award-winning author and philosopher, came to the UK from Kazakhstan in 1993. With a rich background as a science teacher, translator of books, legal cases and NHS interpreter, she channels her diverse experiences and insights into the science fiction genre, exploring the depths of what she has learned and understood throughout her journey.

Subscribe for an Email list: <u>www.ankatroitsky.com</u>

Novels:

- ACT & VIST (- 1) short prequel
- OBJECT & VIST (1)
- CONSTRUCT & VIST (2)
- VIST & PROPER GANDA (3)

Part in Anthology:

- 2024 Next Generation Short Story Awards Anthology of Winners
- Borne in the Blood
- The Dragon's Hoard 2